Stumptown

Stumptown

A. M. Huff

JaMarque Publishing

ISBN: 0966785364
ISBN-13: 978-0966785364

Cover Design by J Caleb Design

CONTENTS

DEDICATION

To my dear friend and sister-in-law,
Pamela Bainbridge-Cowan.

ACKNOWLEDGMENTS

Special thanks to Barbara Larin-Blair, Ruth Bradley, Jonathan Eaton, Chris Forcier, Anthony Huff, Pushpa Huff, Phyllis Jensen, Betsy Jones, Michael Anne Maslow, Kathleen Mooney, Bill Ray and Lea Sevey for their encouragement and support.

CHAPTER ONE

Colorful lights pulsated and spun above the dance floor in time with the loud music. Stumptown, the favorite Friday night hangout of Justus Reynolds and his four friends, was practically dead. Only half the usual crowd was out.

"Where are they?" Dale asked while he looked at the door for the umpteenth time.

"Maybe they aren't coming," Justus answered. He took another sip of his spiced rum and Coke.

"No, they're always here," Dale said and shook his head.

Justus and his four friends were an eclectic group. The one Justus had known the longest was Dale. They lived on the same street and had gone to the same high school, though Dale was a year ahead. They had not been friends back then.

Justus had never suspected Dale's orientation. Dale was the poster boy for straight jocks with his broad shoulders and narrow waist. He lifted weights and ran laps. He played on the basketball team, hung out with the tough guys and even dated

1

one of the cheerleaders. His kind beat up the boys like Justus.

It was not until after graduation that Dale came out, or was thrust out, after he was busted for an *indiscretion* in the men's room of a Fred Meyer store in Tigard. After reading about it in the local paper, Justus ran into Dale on the street. Dale apologized for the way he had treated Justus and the two had become friends.

Even though Dale was barely a year and a couple months older than Justus, who was the youngest of the group at twenty-two, they all teased Dale, calling him *Daddy*. Justus told Dale it was because he seemed more serious and tended to worry and fuss all the time. Dale was quick to point out that Marcus was two months older than him and Jack was actually the oldest since he was twenty-seven.

Dale and Justus had both met Jack at the same time. Justus had been helping Dale move into an apartment off NW 22nd Avenue on Flanders in Portland. It was the first place Dale had been able to find after being thrown out of his parents' house following *the incident*, as Dale's parents referred to it. Justus was helping move Dale's box spring mattress when it became stuck in the stairwell. Dale was trapped at the top while Justus was pinned at the bottom between the wall and mattress, unable to move. Jack had come up the stairs like a knight in shining armor. Between Dale and him, they were able to free the mattress and Justus and get the box springs into Dale's apartment. As luck would have it, Jack was Dale's new neighbor across the hall. He had just passed the Bar Exam and was a lawyer at a small law firm in the trendy Pearl District.

On the other hand, Marcus had been one of the first guys Justus met at Stumptown. Justus had heard of the nightclub through ads in Willamette Week and counted down the days until he was twenty-one. He was nervous walking into the club alone. The doorman did not help, questioning him over and over about his ID before finally letting Justus in.

Stumptown was everything Justus had imagined: bright colorful lights, loud danceable music, and wall-to-wall men. It did not take long before Justus noticed that he seemed to be the youngest person there. He bought the cheapest drink he knew, a rum and Coke, and settled into a chair at a corner table to watch.

Then in walked Marcus. His blonde hair glowed like a halo in the lights. He had a thin, neatly trimmed beard and mustache. He smiled and greeted everyone he saw, waving at others across the club. The bartender seemed to know what Marcus drank and handed a glass to him without Marcus having to place an order. *I want to be like him.*

Justus could not remember how long he had been sitting in the corner, nursing his one drink before Marcus spotted him. He walked over to the table.

"Mind if I sit down?" he asked.

"Sure, go ahead," Justus answered, trying to sound calm and relaxed.

"I haven't seen you here before," Marcus said and flashed a smile. Justus noticed his perfect teeth and lips.

"It's my first time," Justus admitted. "Today's my twenty-first birthday, actually."

That was all the invitation Marcus needed. Justus did not have to buy another drink for the rest of the night. Marcus bought him a "real drink" and led him around the nightclub, introducing him to all his friends and acquaintances. The two danced awhile before returning to their corner table. Justus still felt nervous, or the alcohol was kicking in. They sat, shoulder to shoulder, watching the crowded dance floor while sipping on their drinks. Then suddenly, Marcus shifted in his chair and turned toward Justus. Their eyes met and Marcus leaned closer.

Their mouths met. Justus closed his eyes and wrapped his arms around Marcus' shoulders pulling him closer. He felt every inch of his skin come alive and tingle. It was his first kiss and Justus and never wanted it to stop.

The next morning Justus woke up next to Marcus. He did not remember leaving the club, but he remembered everything else. He looked at Marcus lying next to him and felt a feeling he had never felt before. *Could I be in love?*

Minutes later, Marcus woke up. Without a word or even a glance in Justus' direction, he jumped out of bed, showered, and went downstairs to make coffee. The magic of the moment vanished. Alone in the shower, Justus realized that for Marcus the previous night had been nothing more than a one-night stand, a hookup. The kiss was just part of the game.

It took a few weeks for Justus to get over his broken heart and for Marcus to move into the friend zone, but it happened eventually.

"There's Scotty," Dale announced, pulling Justus out of his thoughts.

Justus looked across the dance floor and spotted Scotty standing beside the front door. "Yoo-hoo," Justus stood up and called out. He waved to Scotty.

Scotty ducked his head and began making his way over to them.

Eugene Brodie was Scotty's real name, but no one called him that except his family. He earned the nickname, Scotty, because he was a Trekkie and had red hair. He was a print technician for Qwik Print two blocks from the U.S. Bancorp Tower where Justus worked. He and Justus had met when Justus was in a hurry to have some copies made for Harrison on the day when both the printers in Justus' office were being serviced.

As it turned out, Scotty was a few months older than Justus. He was very quiet, almost prudish. He had a one-bedroom condo in the Grandview on SW 14th Avenue and walked to work. In fact, Scotty walked everywhere or took TriMet.

It took several months of Justus' coaxing to get Scotty to join the gang on Friday nights and several more months before Scotty learned to relax a bit. Part of the problem, as Scotty confided in Justus one day, was that he was still a virgin. He did not believe in hooking up just for fun. He said it was the way he was raised. "Sex was something you waited until you were married to do and then only with your mate."

"But how will you find a husband if you don't put out?" Justus had asked, to which Scotty only shrugged his shoulders.

"What took you so long?" Justus asked and gave Scotty a welcoming hug once Scotty reached the group's usual table. Justus moved over to the empty chair between Dale and the half-wall that separated the dance floor from the seating area.

"Long day," he answered. He pulled out a chair and sat down.

"Good to see you," Dale said, sounding a bit distracted and on edge. He gulped down the last of his Jack Daniels on ice.

A bare-chested man with six-pack abs holding a small round tray appeared over Dale's shoulder. In the ever-changing colored lights, it was hard to tell the true shade of the man's frosted hair, but Justus still felt his heart flutter.

"Can I get you something from the bar?" he asked. His voice was deep and sultry, the kind that made Justus' knees weak.

"Coke is fine," Scotty said, barely loud enough to be heard over the blaring music.

"Great, and you?" He looked at Justus.

"A Captain Morgan's and Coke."

"And another Jack for you?" he asked Dale.

"Please," Dale answered and grinned.

"Coming right up."

Dale turned in his chair and watched the server return to the bar.

"Okay, put it back in your pants," Justus snipped and took a sip of his own drink while the stirrings in his loins waned.

Dale turned around.

"So now all we're waiting for are Marcus and Jack," Justus said. He glanced at the door again.

"Speaking of Jack," Dale spoke up. "Have either of you seen or heard from him?"

Justus glanced at Scotty and shook his head. "No. Why?"

"Because I haven't seen him since the Valentine's Party two weeks ago," Dale answered.

"Not even in your apartment building?" Scotty asked.

"No. I ran into the mailman the other day who asked about him because Jack's mailbox was full."

"Come to think about it, both of you guys didn't show up last week for our Friday night. Where were you?"

Dale started to answer when the handsome server returned with their drinks. He placed a white cocktail napkin on the table in front of each of them. After they handed him their money, he set their drinks on them. Dale pulled out his wallet and held up his money.

The server smiled and put his hand over Dale's. "Keep it. It's on the house," he said with a wink.

"Are you sure?" Dale asked. When the server nodded Dale handed him a five. "Then this is for you."

"I hope that's not all I get," he replied, while he slipped the money down the front of his apron-wrapped jeans.

Dale's mouth dropped open and then he smiled. The waiter

turned around and left.

"Oh, my, God, did you see that?" Dale gasped.

"Yeah, yeah," Justus groaned. "So, back to Jack. The night of the party was crazy. The last time I saw him he was dancing with some guy. I left so I don't know what happened after that."

"Yeah, I saw who you left with," Dale quipped. "What about you, Scott?"

"Don't look at me. I left before Justus, remember? And now that I think about it, Jack hasn't brought anything to the shop. He's normally by about two or three times a week."

The entrance door opened again and the people nearest the doors came alive. Their voices rose above the loud music.

"Marcus is here," Scotty said and sat up a bit straighter. He smiled and watched Marcus make his way through the small gathering.

Justus noticed the change in Scotty's demeanor. It spoke volumes. Scotty and Marcus had a strange friendship. Marcus was forever teasing Scotty, calling him a prude and telling him he needed to loosen up and get laid. Scotty quietly took it. However, once Scotty had surprised everyone when he told Marcus, "Better a prude than a regular at the free clinic." Marcus had just laughed and the two continued their little banter.

"Hi guys!" Marcus greeted the table when he finally made it across the club. He pulled out the empty chair and sat down beside Scotty. He leaned over and kissed Scotty's cheek, which made Scotty blush and look as though he were about to die.

The server returned and not so shyly leaned against Dale's shoulder. Dale looked up at him and smiled.

"Can I get you something from the bar?" he asked Marcus and tried not to smile.

"I'll have a Tequila Sunrise," Marcus answered.

"Perfect, be right back."

Again, Dale turned and watched the server retreat back to the bar.

"So, what are you all talking about?" Marcus asked and waved at someone across the room.

"Dale was asking if anyone has heard from or seen Jack lately," Justus answered.

Marcus frowned and shook his head. "I haven't. In fact, I tried calling him at work this morning and the receptionist said he hasn't shown up for two weeks. She said to tell him if he doesn't show up for work Monday to forget it. The boss says he's fired."

"Fired?" Scotty gasped.

"Oh no," Dale said and slumped in his chair. "That job means everything to him. He loves it."

"Where could he be?"

"Here you go," the server interrupted and set the bright yellow and orange drink down in front of Marcus. He smiled and let his hand brush against Dale's shoulder. "You need another?" he asked Dale.

"No, I'm fine for now," Dale answered.

When the server left, Marcus grinned. "Somebody's gonna get laid tonight!"

Dale glanced over his shoulder and then looked at them. "You really think?"

"Come off it, Dale. Even Scotty isn't that naïve, no offense Scott," Marcus scoffed.

Scotty's mouth dropped open but then he closed it and went back to nursing his very-diluted soft drink.

"So, what are we going to do about Jack?" Dale asked changing the subject.

"What can we do?" Marcus asked.

"I don't know, but we can't just let it go," Dale said.

"Shouldn't we call the police or something?"

"Probably," Justus answered.

"Well, since you were the last to see him, Justus, perhaps you should talk to them," Marcus suggested.

"Fine, I'll do it," he agreed.

At midnight, Scotty left and headed home. Justus sat alone with his drink staring out at the crowd that had already started to pair off. Marcus was sitting off in a corner with his latest conquest. The two were entwined and practically devouring each other. Dale was across the dance floor at the end of the bar, talking with his hot server.

A lone man in the middle of the dated, parquet wood dance floor captured Justus' attention, but not in any romantic sort of way. It was obvious the guy'd had too much to drink. He wiggled and gyrated, then pulled his shirt off and swung it around over his head. One of the bartenders rushed him and grabbed the shirt away before it could become entangled in the lights. The man reeled and fell on the floor. The two exchanged words before the bouncer showed up and escorted the dancer to the time-out area by the door to wait for a taxi.

"That was sure crazy," a man said, causing Justus to jump and nearly sending the ice in his glass flying. "I'm sorry," he quickly added.

His apology would have sounded more sincere without the laughing, Justus thought.

"Mind if I sit down?" he asked.

"No, go ahead," Justus answered. He looked the man over, gray temples, kind eyes, and a nice smile. His shirt was a bit last season but otherwise he was not too bad looking.

"My name's Dean," he said. His voice was a deep baritone that sent Justus' heart fluttering. Dean held out his hand.

Justus shook it and felt the man's firm grip. "Justus," he

introduced himself.

"Can I get you another . . .?"

"Captain Morgan's and Coke."

Dean signaled for the server and ordered another round of drinks for the two of them.

"I have to admit, I've seen you here many times but I never got up the courage to say hi," Dean said.

"Why tonight then?" Justus asked, sounding almost rude.

Dean did not notice, possibly because of the loud music. "I guess when I saw your friends leave and you sitting here all alone, I thought, why not? Plus, I've had a few of these," he said and held up his empty glass.

"You work downtown?" Justus asked, trying to make conversation.

"Yes, well, sort of. I work for a construction company that's remodeling some buildings in the Pearl."

"Oh, a construction worker." Justus' pulse picked up. He leaned over the table a little more.

"What—"

Their drinks arrived. Dean quickly pulled out a small wad of bills and paid the server. Stuffing his money back into his pocket, he looked at Justus.

"What do you do?" he asked and took a sip of his drink.

"Me? I work for an accounting firm on the twenty-eighth floor of the bank tower on Sixth. I'm a file clerk." He said that last part a little softer hoping Dean would not catch it. A file clerk was not as hot as a construction worker. He picked up his drink. "Thank you for this," he said and took a sip.

"So, what do you like to do?" Dean asked.

Justus must have looked shocked and a bit wide-eyed. Dean's expression changed in a flash to embarrassment.

"I mean for fun," he blurted. "Besides your work."

"Oh," Justus laughed and relaxed. He was not averse to telling him what he was into but it was a little soon. "I don't know. Working full-time keeps me pretty busy. I do like coming here and watching people. What about you?"

"Aside from working, I like dancing—though I'm not very good at it. I also like camping and fishing, but I don't get to do that very often."

"Where do you go camping?"

"Central Oregon mostly but Mount Hood and sometimes over on the coast, depending on the weather and my mood. You ever go camping?"

"Once with my family," Justus answered. "We went to the Wilson River. It rained nearly the whole time. I slept in the car while the rest of my family slept in the tent. I hated it."

"Well, you should give it another chance. Maybe with the right company you might find you like it," Dean said and gave Justus a suggestive look.

"I might have to do that," Justus said. The more Dean talked the more Justus found himself opening up to the idea that he could be fun.

"Would it be too forward of me to ask, would you like to get out of here?"

"That depends, where did you have in mind?"

"I have a place not too far from here. . ."

"Sounds good." Justus gulped down the rest of his drink and looked across the club when he stood up. Dale and his new friend were gone. Marcus was nowhere to be seen either.

Dean put his arm around Justus' waist and led him out of the club. The night air was cold but Justus could feel the warmth from Dean's body. They headed down Stark Street toward SW 9th Avenue. When they reached the corner, Dean escorted Justus across Stark. Justus could see his car parked ahead in the middle of the block on 9ᵗʰ. When they reached the sidewalk, Dean turned back up Stark and stopped in front of a doorway.

"Here?" Justus asked, sounding surprised. He looked over his shoulder at the front door of Stumptown across the street.

"Yeah, I have an apartment on the top floor," Dean said while he keyed a security code on the touch pad. The door buzzed and clicked. Dean opened it.

"That's pretty convenient," Justus said while they waited for the elevator.

"Yeah, makes it easy to get to work every day."

"So, do you live here permanently?"

"No, I have a house in Bend. I'm only renting this place while I'm working in town."

The elevator car arrived and the doors opened. Dean held out his hand inviting Justus to enter.

"How long is that?" Justus continued their conversation.

"Another eight months to a year. It's a pretty big job," Dean answered and pushed the button for the top floor.

The elevator stopped on the ninth floor and the doors opened. The hallway was not unlike the hallway in Dale's building. It was fairly wide, enough room for three or four people to walk side-by-side. Nice, shiny, dark-stained wooden doors were spaced out along the walls but none directly across from the other.

Dean led Justus toward the southeast corner. He unlocked the door and opened it. He stepped inside and turned on the lights. Justus entered. Dean's apartment was decorated in a surprisingly comfortable style. *Harrison would love this.* Justus smiled when thought of his friend and landlord. Dean's living room was small but nice. A sofa, coffee table, and chair were set up facing a large flat-screen TV. There were two windows on the east wall that overlooked 9ᵗʰ Avenue near Washington

Street. *Not the most exciting of views.*

When Dean closed the door, it locked with a loud click. Justus turned around. Dean approached him with a smile on his lips and sparkle in his dark-brown eyes. He took Justus in his arms and leaned in for a kiss. Justus turned his head.

"No kissing," he said as Dean's lips pressed against his cheek.

Dean quickly pulled back but still held Justus in his embrace. "Why's that?"

"It complicates things," Justus answered.

"Oh, okay," Dean said. Justus could hear the disappointment in Dean's tone.

"Not on the lips."

Dean smiled. He leaned in and pressed his lips against Justus' neck.

Justus felt his knees go weak.

CHAPTER TWO

Justus woke the next morning with the sun shining in his face and Dean's warm breath against his back. *What have I done?* He never stayed the night. One-night stand was only a term. It did not really mean he actually stayed the whole night. He was supposed to leave once the deed was done and they both were satisfied. *How did this happen?*

Justus started to get up but felt Dean's strong arm squeeze him tighter, pinning him to the bed.

Oh, dear God, now what? He relaxed and lay still. Dean continued to sleep and snuggle Justus' back.

The digital clock on the nightstand beside the bed blinked away the minutes.

This is all Harrison's fault. If he would allow me to bring guests home, none of this would happen. I'd make sure they left.

Why did I let Dean talk me into cuddling afterward? Cuddling, like kissing, never ends well.

The clock blinked 9:00 A.M. and a buzzer blared. Justus

jumped and so did Dean. He rolled over on top of Justus and palmed the clock, shutting off the alarm.

Justus lay on his back looking up at the man on top of him. Dean's dark-brown, gray-streaked hair was mussed. His brown eyes were half-open. He smiled and Justus could not help but smile back all the while wishing Dean would get off him.

"Morning," Dean said and lowered his head.

Justus quickly turned his and Dean planted a soft kiss on his cheek. Dean's chin felt rough against Justus' smooth skin.

"Morning," Justus said and squirmed. "Gotta pee."

"Oh." Dean quickly moved and let Justus go. "First door on the left," he called as Justus pulled his shirt over his head while hurrying away.

Alone in the bathroom, Justus stared at his reflection in the mirror. "You stupid, stupid idiot, how are you going to get away?" An idea flashed in his mind. He flushed the toilet for effect and returned to the bedroom.

"I'm sorry," he apologized and began to dress quickly. "I forgot I have a family thing at, what time is it?"

"A little after nine," Dean answered while he lay on his side, propped up on his elbow, watching Justus.

"At ten," Justus continued his lie. "I'll have just enough time to get home, shower and change clothes. . ."

"You could shower here," Dean offered.

"As tempting as that sounds, I really need clean clothes."

"Okay," Dean relented, seemingly buying Justus' fib. He threw back the covers and pulled on his bathrobe. Justus caught a glimpse of Dean's buff body and for a moment felt a bit of regret for wanting to leave. Dean met Justus at the bedroom door. "I'm glad you spent the night. It was nice holding you."

Justus smiled and felt anxiety growing in his chest. "It was nice," he said for lack of something better to say.

They walked to the apartment door.

"Can we do this again?" Dean asked. "I really enjoyed it."

"Sure," Justus heard himself answer before he realized what he had said.

"Great, I'll call you later then," Dean said and gave Justus a hug before letting him leave.

Call me later? Did I give him my phone number? Damn, did I lose my mind? I've broken all my rules.

Justus hurried to his car and once safely inside, relaxed. *Dean, you were great but, see ya.*

Twenty-five minutes later, Justus parked his car by the curb in front the old Portland Craftsman house he shared with his friend and co-worker Harrison Andrews. Actually, it was Harrison's house and Justus had sort of made himself at home there a year ago when he was asked to house-sit. However it happened, this was now home.

The morning paper was still on the front porch. He picked it up and then decided it was better to leave it and let Harrison get it. Explaining why he brought it in would be too complicated. Normally he would be in his bedroom upstairs, asleep until nearly noon.

Quietly he slid his key into the lock on the front door and gave it a turn. The heavy wooden door creaked softly when Justus opened it. He cringed and hoped Harrison would not hear. Closing the door behind him, he locked the dead bolt and turned around.

"Well, you're a little late," Harrison greeted him from the dining room.

Justus yelled and jumped back into the door, hitting his head.

"Sorry, didn't mean to startle you," Harrison apologized and covered his grin with his hand. "So, just getting home?"

"Don't ask," Justus grumbled. He rubbed the back of his head and walked over to the table. "Coffee ready?"

"Of course," Harrison answered and turned around. "It's in the kitchen."

Justus followed his housemate into the kitchen. Harrison was older than Justus by nearly ten years. *I wonder how old Dean is? From the back, they could be twins, except Dean has muscles. Harry's a desk jockey. Their hair is about the same color though—oh God, do I have a daddy fixation? No, Harry's too young to be my daddy, but—*

Stop it! Stop thinking like that. That's gross.

"Is something wrong?" Harrison asked while he scooped up scrambled eggs and put them on a platter.

"No, just thinking too much," Justus answered. He grabbed his favorite mug, the one that held nearly two cups, from the cupboard and filled it with coffee, leaving enough room for his sweet cream. Opening the fridge, he did not see it. "Creamer?"

"It's on the table," Harrison answered.

Justus took his coffee and walked around the island in the center of the kitchen. Col. Mustard, Harrison's orange cat, glanced up at him and then returned to eating his own breakfast.

When Justus reached for the cream pitcher in the middle of the table, he noticed the two place settings. He knew the second one was not meant for him since he always sat across from Harrison at the other end of the table.

"Company?" he asked when Harrison set the platter on the table.

"Yes, Doug is washing up."

Justus grinned. "Oh, I see," he said in a suspicious tone.

"No, it's not like that. Doug only dropped by this morning."

"Uh-huh," Justus continued to tease. "It's okay if you two want the house to yourselves for a bit. I can find something to do. . ."

"Sit down," Harrison said in an exasperated tone. "I'll get you a plate."

"I thought I heard your voice," Douglas said when he walked into the dining room.

"Morning, handsome," Justus greeted. Douglas was more to his tastes: rugged and firm body, slightly graying ginger hair on his head and chest, and the hottest blue eyes. Plus, he was straight, a challenge. Justus had to remind himself that Douglas was Thomas' friend.

"Morning to you too, dear," Douglas teased back.

"Don't encourage him," Harrison said, before returning to the kitchen.

"Just get in?" Douglas asked. He grabbed the back of the chair to the right of Harrison's and leaned against it.

Justus could not help looking at Douglas' big hands. For a moment he was lost in his head and then realized he was staring.

"Oh, yeah," Justus answered and shrugged a bit.

"Thought you had a rule about spending the night with someone?"

"I do," Justus answered and shook his head. "Believe me, it wasn't on purpose. Chalk it up to too much to drink."

"I see." Douglas pulled out his chair and sat down when Harrison returned with a plate of toast and another place setting.

He handed the plate and silverware across the table to Justus. Justus jumped up and took them and set them down. He was not really hungry. In fact, he felt a little nauseated, but he enjoyed looking at Douglas.

"So, how are your friends?" Harrison asked.

"Okay, I guess," Justus answered. He watched the two of them dish up their breakfast and decided he would have a piece of toast after all.

"That didn't sound good," Douglas spoke up. "What's wrong?"

"Nothing—well, Dale is worried because Jack is missing."

"What?" Harrison's fork slipped from his fingers and fell onto his plate with a loud clank.

"Dear God, not again," Douglas gasped. He and Harrison exchanged looks.

"No, no, it's not like Thomas," Justus said, remembering the ordeal Harrison and Douglas had gone through nearly a year ago. "Jack was at the club on Valentine's Day and he left with some guy, at least we think he did."

"How is that not like Thomas?" Harrison asked. Justus could hear the fear in his voice.

"I don't know, because he's here and not in Ellensburg?" Justus could not help notice the way Douglas closed his eyes when he said the name of the coastal Oregon town. It had slipped his mind that Douglas' wife Barbara had been murdered by the crooked cops in that town. "I'm sorry," he apologized.

Douglas did not respond, apparently lost in a memory.

"So, wha—Why do you think he's missing?" Harrison asked.

"Dale," Justus started again but kept an eye on Douglas. "He's a friend from high school—"

"Yes, we know," Harrison urged.

"Well, he and Jack are neighbors. Last night Dale mentioned he hadn't seen Jack in a long time. Marc—"

Harrison nodded that he and Douglas knew who Marcus was.

"Marcus told us he called Jack's work and was informed that Jack hadn't been in in two weeks and was about to lose his job."

"Is this normal for him?" Harrison asked.

Justus shrugged. "Dale didn't think so. He's really worried."

"So why are you so upset? I mean, he sounds like he's more Dale's friend than yours," Harrison asked.

"I think I was the last one of the group to see him. So the guys think I should be the one to go to the police." Justus looked at Douglas. He sat staring at his coffee, not eating or saying a word.

"Do you want me to go with you?" Harrison asked, but the tone of his voice seemed to beg Justus to say no.

"Nah, I think I can do it on my own. Besides, you two probably need some alone time." He smirked, looking at Douglas but Douglas did not react. "Are you okay?" Justus reached across the table and touched Douglas' hand.

Douglas looked at him. His blue eyes were shiny with tears. He forced a smile and nodded.

"I didn't mean to upset you," Justus said.

"You didn't," Douglas answered with a gravelly voice.

After a few more awkward attempts at conversation, Justus apologized to Douglas again for mentioning Ellensburg. He poured a fresh cup of coffee, excused himself and went upstairs.

Moments later, standing in the upstairs shower with hot water pouring over his body, he played back in his mind what had happened downstairs. *Stupid, stupid, stupid! Why did you have to bring up Ellensburg? That was so insensitive.* After a rather long shower and an even longer self-reprimand, Justus dressed and came back down the stairs.

"You're still here?" he said when he saw Douglas and Harrison sitting in the living room. The TV in the corner was on but Justus did not recognize the program.

"I was about to ask you the same thing," Douglas fired back. His mood seemed to have lifted and he was back to his teasing self.

"Well, I'm leaving," Justus answered.

"Hey, I was meaning to ask you how that old car of yours is running?" Douglas asked.

"Fine, it works great, no problems. Thanks again for fixing it."

"Anytime," Douglas answered. "If you ever go to trade it in, let me take a look at it to be sure it's in tip-top shape."

"That's not gonna happen for a long time. When dad gave it to me, he called it a *family heirloom.* So I'm stuck with the beast until either it falls apart or dad dies, knock on wood." Justus knocked on the wall.

"You do know that's plaster," Douglas teased.

Justus looked at the wall.

"Speaking of your parents, how do they like Arizona?" Harrison asked.

"Dad loves it. He plays golf every day. Mom hates it. She misses my sister and me."

"Have you ever thought about visiting them, maybe permanently?" Harrison teased even though his tone sounded serious. At least Justus thought he was teasing.

"Oh, hell no! They have snakes, scorpions, and big creepy bugs down there." Justus shuddered. "Plus, I'd hate to leave you. You need me." He gave Harrison an air kiss.

"Like a bad headache," Harrison muttered under his

breath.

"Before you go," Douglas spoke up. "Do you know where your friend Jack lives?"

"Yes. Why?"

"Well, if he lives in the city, you should go to the Portland police. If he's outside the city limits and in Multnomah County, you would want to go to the sheriff's office."

"Oh," Justus answered and then furrowed his brow, a telltale sign that he was searching the files in his head. "He lives near NW 22nd and Flanders."

"City Police then," Harrison and Douglas said at the same time.

"You should try the police station at the jail building downtown," Harrison suggested.

"Why's that?"

"Because the policewoman at the one close to work wasn't too helpful last year."

"Okay." Justus nodded.

"Do you have a picture of Jack?" Douglas asked. "You'll need to give them a recent one."

Justus pulled out his cell phone. "Got it."

"Good. Let us know how it goes and if you need anything, give me a call," Harrison said.

"Will do, dad," Justus teased. "Now, you two behave yourselves. Don't do anything I wouldn't do."

"That leaves it open." Douglas laughed.

"Just remember to keep the noise down. You don't want the neighbors to hear."

Harrison's eyebrows lowered. "Go on!" he said.

"Bye! And that's not my sexual preference," Justus teased. He closed the front door behind him and continued to laugh all the way to his car.

CHAPTER THREE

The knot in Justus' stomach had not loosened all weekend. After submitting the missing person report, the officer explained that, should they locate Jack and his actions were voluntary, they might not be able to disclose his whereabouts unless he gave the police permission to do so. "Filing a missing person report on an adult doesn't entitle you to know where they are, only that they are safe," she had said.

Why did I even bother? Justus had the feeling he had wasted his time and that the police were not really going to do anything. He wondered if this was how Harrison felt last year when Thomas had disappeared.

Adding to his discomfort was the fact he had been avoiding Dean's phone calls, and there were many, sometimes one right after the other. He did listen to the messages, which did not help matters because Dean sounded so happy and hopeful. *Why doesn't he take the hint?*

"Cheer up," Harrison said when they reached the twenty-eighth floor. "Remember, focus on work."

"That's easy for you to say," Justus said.

"I know," Harrison answered. "But give the police a chance to do their thing."

"There you are," a woman greeted when Justus and Harrison walked into the main office. "I left you something on your desk."

"What?" Justus asked and turned around to see her slip out the door heading for her office downstairs.

"Wonder what that was all about?" Harrison said.

"Me too," Justus said and picked up his pace.

The file room was a windowless room right inside the main office doors. It had an open archway instead of doors, something that Justus did not understand given the sensitive files stored in the cabinets. In the center of the room, two desks had been pushed together, facing each other. They were separated by a small cloth-covered partition that sat along the front edges of the desks. It was the width of the desk and a foot high. Large, metal filing cabinets lined the walls. The cabinets to the right were white, against the far wall, gray, and to the left, black. At first Justus thought they were color coded based on the files inside, but he quickly learned the color had nothing to do with the filing system. A large schoolhouse-style clock hung above the cabinets on the wall opposite the doorway. Its mechanism was synced with the other clocks in the outer office. Debra, his former workmate, had accused Justus of ducking out early to their boss. She had always been trying to get people fired. It turned out that she had tampered with the clock. Regardless, in the end, she had been the one who lost her job.

Justus stopped abruptly in the doorway when he saw the *something* on his desk. Harrison bumped into him.

"Well, well, well," he said and put his hand on Justus' shoulder. "Guess you were either really good or really bad," he teased and laughed.

Justus scowled at him. He knew who had sent them. There was only one person who would have. *How did he know where I worked? Did I tell him?*

"So, who are they from?" Harrison asked and slipped past Justus. He walked over to the flowers and took the small card off the plastic fork stuck in the center of the bouquet.

"Don't!" Justus gasped, sounding afraid.

Harrison looked at him and laughed. "Why? What's wrong?"

"I know who sent them," he answered.

"You do?"

"Yes, it's the guy I spent the night with," Justus admitted.

"I thought you weren't supposed to tell people where you worked. Isn't that one of your rules?"

"Yes," Justus answered sounding disgusted with himself. "It just slipped out. Would you take them away, please?"

"What do you want me to do with them?"

"I don't know, keep them or give them to someone. I don't care. I don't want to see them."

"Then I'll give them to Vicki since she brought them up."

"Fine," Justus answered.

Harrison picked up the vase and started to leave. He stopped and handed Justus the small envelope. "At least read the message," he said in a fatherly tone.

Justus took the envelope. Harrison left. Slowly Justus walked over to his desk. He opened the unsealed flap and pulled out a small card. "Have a good day, Dean," it read. He stuck the card back into the envelope and dropped it into the wastebasket under his desk.

When Justus rounded the corner of SW 9th Avenue onto Stark Street, he could hear the excited chatter of a group of guys headed for Stumptown. Judging by the lack of parking for two blocks around the club, it promised to be a good night. He opened the heavy, carved wood door and immediately the music spilled into the street.

Once his eyes adjusted to the dim light, Justus spotted the gang at their usual table. Dale waved him over.

"Hey where've you been?" Dale asked. "Normally you're the first one here." He gave Justus a bear hug.

Justus pulled out an empty chair over to the table and sat down between Dale and Scotty, facing the dance floor. He glanced at Marcus, seated on the other side of Scotty against the rail divider. Marcus was distracted by someone on the dance floor.

"May I get you something from the bar?" a voice spoke into Justus' ear, causing him to jump.

Justus looked at the server. He recognized him immediately as the guy Dale had hooked up with the week before, only now neither would look at the other.

"Uh, sure, a Captain Morgan's and Coke, heavy on the rum," Justus answered.

"Coming right up," the server said and gave Justus a pat on his shoulder before disappearing into the crowd.

"Busy night," Justus said, almost having to shout over the loud music and chatter.

"Live DJ night," Scotty shouted back. He pointed toward the head of the dance floor at the large speakers and console that had been set up.

That explains the added volume, Justus thought.

The server returned and set Justus' drink down in front of

him. Justus paid for the drink and gave him a tip. The server thanked him, glared at Dale for a moment then left.

"I take it the romance is over?" Justus asked Dale.

Dale shot a glance over his shoulder in the direction of the bar and then turned back to his friends. "Yeah, and it was so promising, too. How could someone so hot be so lousy in bed?"

"What?" Marcus gasped, glanced at the bar and then back at Dale. "You not talking about Troy are you?"

"Yes," Dale answered.

"You're nuts! What do you mean? He's an animal," Marcus said in the server's defense. "It must have been you."

Dale glared at Marcus and pursed his lips as though getting ready to punch him.

"Never mind him," Scotty interrupted. "Any news on Jack?"

Justus' shoulders slumped a bit. He looked at his drink. He really did not want to talk about Jack even though he could not get Jack out of his head. He took a gulp of his drink and almost choked. It was a lot stronger than he had expected.

"I made the report last Saturday," he finally said. "The policewoman said they'd look into it but not to get my hopes up. If Jack doesn't want to be found we may never know where he went or why, or if he intends on coming back."

"Well, thanks but no thanks," Marcus quipped. He gulped down the rest of his drink, leaving only ice cubes to melt away.

"What's the good of filing a report then?" Scotty asked.

"She did say when they find him they could at least let us know if he's okay."

"Well, that's something, I guess." Dale sighed and slumped in his chair a bit.

"So, now what?" Scotty asked.

"Well, I don't know about you guys, but I'm going to get another drink and have a look around," Marcus responded. "There are some really hot guys out tonight and some new faces."

"Who are you kidding, you aren't looking at faces," Dale teased.

"Very funny," Marcus said while he stood up. Before anyone could object, he disappeared in the crowd.

"He's such a whore," Dale said.

"Don't call him that!" Scotty snapped. "You're not exactly innocent."

"Well excuse me, Virgin Scotty."

"Enough!" Justus shouted. "Will you two stop it already?"

"Well, he started it," Dale said.

"No, you started it by calling Marcus a whore," Scotty snapped again.

"I don't care," Justus said. "None of us, except you Scotty, have any room to talk."

"That's right." Scotty sneered at Dale.

"Fine, I'm outta here." Dale stood up and was gone.

"Some things never change," Scotty said. He shook his head and took a sip of his drink.

"We should cut him some slack," Justus said. "He's worried about Jack."

"No, he's being a jerk, as usual," Scotty groused.

"What on earth have you been drinking tonight?" Justus asked. "This is a new side of you."

"It's just Coke," Scotty admitted and tilted his glass to show Justus its dark-liquid contents. "Sometimes he gets on my nerves, that's all."

"I see. Well, nice to hear you speaking up," Justus said

and bumped shoulders with him.

"Mind if I join you guys?" Dean asked and slipped into Dale's abandoned chair before either Justus or Scotty could answer.

"Hi," Justus gasped and felt his body go numb. "What are you doing here?"

"What everyone else is, I guess," he answered and smiled while he looked at Justus.

"Oh yeah," Justus said.

"So, who's your friend?" Scotty asked.

Justus glanced at Scotty and felt panicked. Reluctantly, he introduced the two.

"Nice to meet you, Scotty," Dean said politely. "I'm glad I ran into you." He looked back at Justus. "So how was your week?"

"Crazy."

"Did you get the flowers?"

"Flowers?" Scotty asked.

Justus glanced at him and then back at Dean. "Yes, thank you," he acknowledged.

"I was wondering because you haven't returned my calls."

Scotty drank the last of his Coke and stood up. "I'm gonna get another Coke," he announced and slipped away.

Without his backup, Justus felt himself growing more anxious. "I'm sorry," he said, feeling cornered. "A lot has been going on. One of our friends is missing."

"Oh my, I'm sorry. What happened?" Dean asked sounding sincere.

"We don't know. He was last seen leaving the Valentine's Day party with some guy."

"I see."

The conversation died quietly. Justus looked across the dance floor at the bar where Scotty stood with his fresh glass of Coke. Justus realized he was not coming back.

"Say, I was wondering if you wanted to get out of here and come up to my place?" Dean asked.

"I just got here," Justus answered and shook his head. "I'd sort of like to stick around."

"Okay, maybe later then?" Dean's tone sounded hopeful.

"We'll see," Justus said and immediately the image of his father flashed in his head. Whenever Justus' father or mother said those words it meant no. Justus cringed inside at the thought that he had turned into his parents. "I'll be right back."

Before Dean could say another word, Justus practically leapt from his chair. "I gotta pee," he said. He left his drink behind and slipped into the crowd. Keeping up his pretense, he headed for the men's room where he hoped to find an empty stall so he could hide out.

Pushing on the swinging door to the hallway, he glanced over his shoulder to make sure Dean was not following. The door struck something with a loud thud. Justus quickly jumped back and pulled the door open.

"I'm so sorry," he apologized to the man leaning against the wall rubbing his forehead. "Did I hurt you?"

"No," the man answered and laughed. "Something wrong?" he asked and looked past Justus, through the small window in the door, at the bar.

Justus gave the stranger the head-to-crotch once over: fabulous light brown hair, piercing dark eyes, nice beard and mustache, and a body screaming to get out of those clothes. Justus smiled at his new conquest. "Yeah, I'm trying to get away from someone."

The man smiled and leaned closer. "Name's Barry," he

said into Justus' ear.

"Justus."

"Well Justus, you ran into the right person. Come with me. I know a place we can go where that guy won't find you."

"Sure," Justus said. *I'd follow you anywhere.*

Barry turned around and headed back down the hall toward the restrooms.

"The men's room?" he asked Barry.

"You'll see."

Barry stopped at a door across from the men's room and looked back up the short hallway.

"The maintenance closet?" Justus asked.

Barry laughed a deep hearty laugh. Justus felt his knees weaken a bit. "No," he answered and pushed the door open revealing a small room with a cot. Justus' pulse quickened. "This is the room they use for people who get sick or need to lay down for a bit."

"You're serious?" Justus asked. In his brief one year of being allowed in bars and clubs he had never heard of such a room. Before Barry could answer, he rushed into the room and sat down on the cot. Barry let the door close.

The look in Barry's eyes sent chills through Justus' body. Justus glanced at the small side table and under the dimly lit lamp noticed a small bowl of condoms in gold wrappers.

"You sure we won't be interrupted?" he asked and looked at Barry.

Barry smiled and turned the knob on the dead bolt. "Door's locked," he answered.

The music from the dance floor masked the sounds coming from the small room. Barry was right; with the door locked they were able to satisfy each other without interruption.

"That was amazing," Justus said while he lay in the

afterglow with Barry partly lying next to him, partly on him.

"It was," Barry agreed.

"Do you bring lots of guys back here?"

"No, you're the first."

Justus did not believe him. Barry knew too much about the room for this to be his first time. Justus wiggled free and started to get dressed.

"Don't you want to lay here a bit?" Barry asked.

"Oh, I would but I'm with some friends. I'm sure they're wondering what happened to me," Justus answered, pretending as best he could that he really wanted to stay.

Barry jumped up and started getting into his clothes. "If you wait, I'll walk out with you."

"That's okay. It might be better if we leave separately." Justus stepped into his shoes and finished buttoning his shirt before unlocking the door. "I'll see you on the outside," he said then slipped back into the hall.

He was about to push on the swinging door when the door burst inward. Justus jumped back a step.

"Oh, there you are," Dean said with a smile. "I thought you might have left or something. You said you were coming back."

Justus thought quickly. "I wasn't feeling too good."

The sound of a door opening behind them caused Dean to look past Justus. Dean's smile disappeared. Justus glanced over his shoulder. Barry was still doing up his belt, and his shirt was half untucked. He froze when he saw the two.

"Come on, I'll get you a drink," Dean said and took Justus by the arm. Justus could not read Dean's tone but the tight grip Dean had on his arm made him nervous.

"I'm good, really," he declined while being pulled back into the club's main room.

"A drink might help you feel better," Dean insisted, leaning closer to Justus' ear.

The music seemed louder. Dean escorted Justus up to the bar, still holding onto his arm with a tight grip. He leaned across the bar and ordered two drinks. When the bartender returned, he let go of Justus' arm to retrieve his wallet from his back pocket. Justus seized the opportunity and slipped away.

He did not stop running until he reached his car. He fumbled with his keys, nearly dropping them. Once he unlocked the driver's door, he slipped inside and locked it securely behind him.

Dear God, that was close.

He put the key in the ignition and drove away. Once safely across the Burnside Bridge, he pulled over and took out his phone. He sent Scotty, Dale, and Marcus a text explaining he had to leave and would talk to them later. All except for Marcus responded. Justus figured Marcus was otherwise occupied. Still shaking, Justus headed home.

It took twenty minutes to get through all of the traffic lights on Sandy before turning east onto Halsey. His hands gripped the steering wheel so tightly his fingernails dug into his palms. He could not remember when he had ever felt so frightened.

He turned north on 62nd Avenue before he slowed down. When he came to Broadway, he turned right and parked at the curb. It took all his strength to release the steering wheel and even then his hands shook. Before unlocking the car door, he turned and looked behind him to be sure he was not followed.

"You're sure home early," Harrison greeted him when he came rushing into the house. Justus closed the front door and locked it behind him.

Harrison stood in the foyer, a fresh glass of wine in his

hand and a confused, yet concerned, look on his face.

Justus lunged at Harrison and wrapped his arms around him.

"What is it? What's wrong?" Harrison asked while he held onto Justus' trembling body.

Justus did not answer. His throat tightened and tears began to seep through his tightly shut eyelids.

Justus woke the next morning with the sunlight shining through his window. The aroma of bacon and freshly brewed coffee reached his nose. *Harrison's awake.* Justus threw off the covers and grabbed his robe. He headed down to the kitchen.

"Morning," Harrison greeted. He stood facing the stove with his back to the foyer.

"Morning," Justus returned. He took his coffee mug from the cupboard and filled it.

"Feeling better this morning?" Harrison asked.

"A little," Justus said and poured cream into his dark brew, turning it to a medium brown shade. He walked around the island and pulled out a stool, then sat down. The memory of last night was still vivid and so were the emotions. His hand shook when he raised his mug to take a sip of his coffee. He set the mug down.

"So, do you want to tell me what happened?" Harrison asked.

"It was nothing really," Justus answered.

Harrison turned around and looked at him. His expression told Justus he did not believe him.

"I don't know," Justus said and looked away.

"Maybe it will help if you talked about it," Harrison said.

Justus looked up. He remembered last year, when Thomas moved out, that Harrison had slipped into a silent depression. No matter how much Justus had tried to pull him out of it, Harrison stayed locked away in his head. In the end, Harrison had to be the one to get himself out.

"Fine," Justus relented, knowing that Harrison was not going to give up on him as easily as Justus had given up on Harrison a year ago. "I ran into Dean last night."

"Aha," Harrison said and nodded. He turned back to the stove and stirred the scrambled eggs.

"He was a bit too clingy and he caught me with another guy when I slipped away to use the restroom."

"What?" Harrison gasped and stopped scooping the eggs onto the plater. "You weren't making out in the bathroom, were you?"

"No. It was in a maintenance closet."

"Oh my god," Harrison said and shook his head.

"Well, you asked," Justus said. He felt himself rising out of his anxiety. He smiled at Harrison's expression. "Dean didn't actually walk in on us. He saw Barry come of the closet—" He chuckled at the pun. "When he saw Barry, it was obvious what had happened."

"I see." Harrison returned the frying pan to the cooling range top.

"Dean was—I don't know, not happy. He grabbed my arm and insisted I have another drink but I slipped away."

"Well, it's over now," Harrison said, sounding certain.

Justus felt himself slipping. "I hope you're right."

"Let's eat."

Justus looked around the kitchen. Col. Mustard was finished with his breakfast and was now washing his face. The rest of the house was quiet.

"Where's Douglas?" Justus asked and followed Harrison into the dining room.

"Working, I imagine."

"You mean, he's not here?"

"No."

"Is he coming over later?"

"Don't know."

Justus let the conversation drop. Harrison was not biting this morning. *It's no fun teasing when he doesn't play along.*

CHAPTER FOUR

Except for calls from Marcus, Scotty, and Dale wanting to know what happened Friday night at the club, Justus' phone was quiet. No calls from Dean. Not even a text. *Maybe he got the message.* Justus watched the numbers above the door light up while the elevator rose to the twenty-eighth floor. The car stopped, a bell dinged, and the doors slid open.

Justus followed Harrison out and into the office.

"See you at lunch," Harrison called over his shoulder and proceeded to his office.

"It's a date," Justus answered and smiled when he saw Harrison's back stiffening.

He entered the file room and stopped. A numbing chill coursed down his body, causing his legs to feel weak and his feet to become like bricks. He reached out and grabbed the threshold to steady himself.

Sitting on his desk was a single red rose in a vase. A large white envelope was propped up against it with Justus' name written on it in a loopy script.

Justus felt his pulse quicken and his breathing become shallow. *This can't be happening.* He pushed himself away from the doorway and staggered back into the main office. The strength returned to his legs while he crossed the floor to Harrison's office in the corner by the windows.

"He did it again!" Justus announced.

Harrison looked up from reading something on his computer.

"What? Who?"

"Dean," Justus replied. "He sent more flowers."

"What?" Harrison stood up and was heading for the file room before Justus could answer. It was obvious to him that Harrison had heard what he said. Justus followed.

Harrison did not hesitate, walking into Justus' file room and heading straight over to the flower. Without asking, he picked up the envelope and tore it open. Glancing at Justus, he pulled the card out and read the inscription out loud.

"I'm sorry for the way I acted last Friday night. I was stupid and, yes, jealous. It won't happen again, I promise. Love, Dean." Harrison looked at Justus. "That was nice of him."

"That's creepy, you mean."

"What? The guy likes you, what's wrong with that?" Harrison put the card back on the desk.

"I don't know. It gives me the creeps," Justus said and looked at the flower again. "Take it with you, please."

Harrison grabbed the bud vase.

"And the card."

Harrison picked up the card but did not look pleased. He walked over to Justus. "If you don't want this guy, then man up and tell him."

"I've tried," Justus said and felt a little resentful at

Harrison's tone.

"Well, he's not getting the message," Harrison said.

"Duh," Justus answered. He found himself gritting his teeth at the way Harrison sounded like his father.

Harrison took the card and flower and left Justus alone.

Friday came quickly, or at least it seemed like it for Justus. Dean had texted several times but he ignored them. He thought about blocking Dean's number but the uncertainty of how Dean would react scared him.

"Pop!" Dale gasped and grabbed Scotty's glass. "Oh no, no! No wonder you are so uptight. Tonight, you're getting a real drink." He turned around and raised his hand to get the waiter's attention.

The shirtless server stood at a nearby table. He glanced at him and his smile vanished. He flicked his head in a disdainful gesture as though telling Dale to wait his turn.

"We'll get you liquored up and relaxed in no time."

"I really don't want anything," Scotty protested.

"Nonsense."

Justus sat back and sipped his drink while he listened to the two of them. He really was not in the mood to get in the middle of their banter, not yet anyway. Maybe after a couple more drinks.

The waiter sauntered over and Dale ordered a drink for Scotty amid Scotty's objections. When the server returned, he set the drink down in the center of the table. Dale quickly paid for the drink and the server went on his way.

"I'm not drinking that," Scotty objected and reached for his soft drink. Dale pulled it away.

Marcus emerged from the crowd. He rushed over to the table and sat down in the empty chair between Dale and Justus.

"That for me?" he asked and grabbed the drink from the center of the table.

"No!" Dale gasped and reached for the glass but Marcus took a sip and pulled it away.

"That was for Scotty," Dale snapped.

Marcus looked at Scotty with a shocked expression. Scotty shook his head.

"Scotty doesn't drink," Marcus said, glancing back at Dale. "Scotty, may I have your drink?"

"Sure," Scotty answered.

Dale's mouth dropped open in a silent protest.

"You said it was his and he can do with it what he wants," Marcus said and took a long, flaunting sip.

"What are you doing here so early?" Dale sneered.

"Oh, I heard some news and I had to tell you guys," he answered and leaned toward the center of the table. "I just found out another person is missing."

"What?" they all echoed.

"Yeah, some guy named Alexander was last seen leaving Embers over on NW Broadway and Burnside with a dude."

"When was that?" Justus asked.

"It was after their New Year's Eve party."

"And no one has seen him since?" Justus inquired.

"Nope."

"Does anyone know who he left with?" Scotty asked.

"No." Marcus frowned. "His friend said he hadn't seen the guy before or since and doesn't know his name."

"Did his friend go to the police?" Dale asked.

"He did but the Beaverton Police said basically the same thing the Portland Police said."

"Why'd they go to Beaverton?" Dale asked.

"According to his friend, Alexander lives in Beaverton."

"I need another drink," Justus said and stood up. The current conversation was only adding to his anxiety. Before anyone said another word, he stood up, took his empty glass and headed for the bar.

Squeezing between two guys, Justus set his empty glass on the bar and rested his hand near it to signal the bartender.

"What can I get you?" the bartender asked, taking away the empty glass and putting it out of sight under the counter.

"I don't know, surprise me but make it strong," Justus said.

"Got it," the bartender smiled.

"Bad day?" the man beside Justus asked.

Justus turned and looked at him. To his surprise, the man was quite handsome. Dark hair, blue eyes, neatly trimmed beard and mustache, and a nice build: exactly his type.

"Sort of," Justus answered.

"You want to go somewhere quiet and talk about it?" the man asked with that familiar look in his eyes that said they would not be doing a lot of talking.

"Sure, why not," Justus answered.

"Here's your drink," the bartender interrupted.

Justus started to pay for it when the man in front of him beat him to the punch.

"Thank you, but you didn't have to do that."

"I know. I'll consider it an investment."

"Oh, that's smooth." Justus took a sip of his drink. The taste of alcohol was strong, just like he had ordered, but was still more than he expected. It burned his throat and made him give a slight cough.

"What do you say we go to your place?" the man suggested.

"My—Oh, I can't," Justus replied. "My landlord doesn't

allow me to bring anyone home."

"Really? Why does your landlord care?"

"I'm renting a room in his house."

"Oh, that's too bad."

"Why don't we go to your place?" Justus suggested with eager anticipation.

"Can't," he answered and took a gulp of his beer.

That's when Justus spotted the ring on the man's finger. "You're married?"

"Oh!" the guy looked at his hand and laughed. "Guess I forgot to take it off. Sorry about that."

"Me too," Justus answered. "I don't hook up with married men. That's a line I won't cross."

"But—"

"I'm sorry," Justus said. "Those are the rules." He gave the man a last once-over look and sighed before heading back to his friends.

The sun shining through the window awakened Justus. He looked around his bedroom, confused about how he had gotten here. The last thing he remembered had been sitting around the table at Stumptown. He looked at the clock on the small nightstand beside his bed. It read 10:21 AM. He quickly sat up only to have his head throb and feel as if it were going to explode. He leaned forward until the sensation abated.

Slowly he walked down the stairs. The scent of freshly brewed coffee filled the house. He took a deep breath and felt the pounding in his head. Gently, with the poise of Miss America, he walked into the kitchen.

Col. Mustard began mewing loudly and wrapped himself around and between Justus' legs.

"Do you have to do that so loudly?" Justus groaned.

"I thought I heard you up," Harrison greeted, coming into the kitchen from the hallway to Justus' left.

Justus grabbed his head to keep it from coming off. "Loud," he said in a way that sounded more like shut up.

"Coffee?" Harrison offered in a whisper.

Justus did not answer. He pulled out a stool and sat down.

Harrison poured coffee into Justus' large coffee mug and set it on the island.

Justus ignored the creamer and took a sip of the brew.

"You really tied one on last night," Harrison said, pressing his palms flat on the island's smooth top and leaning forward. "Good thing your friends called me."

"They called you?"

"Yes. They weren't about to let you drive in your condition."

Justus looked around the kitchen. "Where's my car?"

"It's out front. Doug drove it home for you."

"Oh, good." Justus relaxed and took another sip of his black coffee before grabbing the creamer.

"Justus, what's going on? This isn't like you."

"I don't know. Last night we found out another guy went missing about six weeks before Jack. He was last seen leaving Embers with some guy. Then this married guy tried to pick me up."

"How did you know he was married?"

Justus held up his left hand and wiggled his ring finger.

"Oh, I see," Harrison said and gave a nod. He took a drink from his coffee cup and then dumped the rest in the sink. Justus watched, but his head throbbed too much for him to focus. Harrison refilled his cup with fresh, steaming coffee. "What about this other guy? Do you know him?"

"Who?"

"The guy who disappeared."

"Oh," Justus answered and grimaced. "No."

"Well, maybe it's a coincidence? Maybe the two aren't related."

"What do you mean?"

"They both disappeared after leaving a gay bar, didn't they?" Harrison asked.

"Yeah," Justus said, trying to focus his thoughts.

"The same bar?" Harrison asked.

"No. Jack was last seen at the Valentine's Day party at Stumptown. Alexander was at Embers' New Year's Eve party."

"You think there may be a connection?"

"I don't know," Harrison answered. "It was only a thought. The police will get to the bottom of it," Harrison said.

Justus took another sip of his coffee and reached for the cream. While his headache subsided, his mind began to think about what Harrison said. He never thought the two were connected. Now, it was all he could think about. *Thanks a lot, Harrison!*

"So, what have you got planned for today?" Harrison asked.

"Why?" Justus asked, giving Harrison a suspicious glance. Harrison never asked him about his plans for Saturday.

"No reason," Harrison said and shrugged his shoulders. "I was going to hang out here in case Dani calls."

"Still haven't heard from her?"

"No," Harrison answered. He glanced at the telephone on the counter behind Justus.

"How long has it been since you heard from her?" Justus asked while he tried to remember when Harrison told him about her going into hiding with her boys.

"It was months ago. I thought she would have contacted

me by now—"

"She's fine," Justus said when he saw Harrison's worried expression.

"I know," Harrison answered. "It's just that her husband is a violent asshole."

"Didn't you say he was in jail?"

"They usually only hold a person for twenty-four hours, but he's a cop. They get special treatment."

"True, but she got away, remember?" Justus tried to sound reassuring.

"I know, but. . ."

Justus felt bad for him. He knew how close Harrison and his sister were and knew this was really bothering him. Still, he could not think of a thing to say to ease his anxiety.

Col. Mustard began meowing in earnest. Justus looked down at the floor at the end of the island. Col. Mustard sat beside his water dish staring up at Harrison. He meowed again.

"I know, I know, I haven't forgotten you," Harrison said. "Hang on, you're not starving."

Col. Mustard mewed sharply.

"Okay, okay, I'm hurrying."

Justus watched while Harrison grabbed a can of cat food from the pantry and began dishing up his pet's breakfast.

CHAPTER FIVE

Justus parked his car on the curb across the street from The Roxy in downtown Portland. He checked his phone for messages before stepping out onto SW Stark. His heart was beating fast. Dean's apartment was two short blocks down the street. It was too close, but Marcus had insisted they meet up at his favorite restaurant. Since he was buying, Justus agreed.

Marcus was seated at a table beneath a movie poster with George Clooney's image. Justus had not seen the movie but thought George was hot. After surveying the nearly empty restaurant and not seeing Dean anywhere, Justus relaxed and slid onto the pew bench. From that vantage point he could see the front door clearly.

"Hi," he greeted Marcus with an air kiss. He noticed another place setting on the table. "Are you expecting someone else?"

"Yeah," Marcus answered. "I called the guys to see if they wanted to join us."

"And?"

"Dale said he was busy but might stop by and Scotty said he'd be here."

"Good," Justus said. He smiled to himself.

A waitress took Justus' drink order and then headed across the room to the lunch counter. Justus watched her while she grabbed a coffee cup and the pot. She set the cup on the table in front of Justus and filled it.

"When you're ready to order, give me a call," she said and returned to her guests at the counter.

"How are you feeling today?" Marcus asked.

"Better," Justus answered.

"You were really out of it last night. I've never seen you that drunk before. What were you drinking?"

"I don't know. I asked the bartender for something strong."

"Well, you got it."

Suddenly Justus felt self-conscious. He could not remember anything from the night before. He felt his cheeks turning red.

"Uh, did I do anything embarrassing last night?" he asked nervously.

"I don't know. You only made out with a guy on the dance floor. You tore off his shirt and then yours and practically raped him."

"No, I didn't!" Justus' face felt hot.

"Yeah, you did. If it wasn't for Scotty dragging you away, Stumptown could have been shut down for indecency." Marcus laughed.

"Oh, God." Justus buried his face in his hands.

Marcus roared and sat back against the wall. "I'm kidding!" he said.

"Seriously?" Justus looked at him.

"Yes. You didn't do anything but pass out at our table after you finished your drink."

"Oh, you!" Justus slapped Marcus on the arm.

"Had you going there for a moment, didn't I?"

"Yes, but it's not funny."

"What's not funny?" Scotty asked and pulled out the only chair at the table. He sat down across from Marcus and looked at them.

"I was teasing Justus about last night," Marcus said.

"Oh." Scotty nodded.

The waitress returned. She took Scotty's drink order, then left and returned with his large class of orange juice. They placed their lunch order and she left again.

"So, what's new?" Scotty asked.

"I have something interesting," Justus spoke up. "This morning I told Harry about the other missing guy. He thinks the disappearance of this guy and Jack could be related."

"Really?" Scotty said, sounding surprised.

"Yeah, they were both last seen leaving gay nightclubs with guys. Maybe it's the same guy?"

"It could be, but no one seems to remember what the other guy looks like. So there's no way of knowing," Marcus spoke up.

"Hey, do you think Stumptown has one of those security cameras like they do at gas station stores?" Scotty asked.

Suddenly Justus felt his face flush again. The thought that someone would have him and Barry on camera left him feeling panicked.

"I doubt it," Marcus answered. "They don't even like people snapping pictures with their cell phones inside. If they see you, they make you delete it. It's highly unlikely they would have their own cameras."

Justus relaxed a little.

The waitress returned with three plates filled with steaming fries and huge cheeseburgers. She set them down on the table in front of them. "Is there anything else?" she asked. "I've got a fresh pot of coffee brewing."

"That would be great," Marcus told her.

Justus watched her return to her station.

"So, what do we do now?" Justus asked.

"Do?"

"Yeah, how do we find Jack?"

"I thought the police were looking," Marcus said.

"They are, but we have to do something."

"How can we do anything when we don't know who is behind it? Or if there even is a who?" Marcus answered.

"I don't know," Justus said. Marcus was right. They needed more information in order to be able to do anything. Perhaps the police were having better luck.

"So, have you heard anymore from that Dean guy?" Scotty asked, changing the subject.

"No, thank heaven. I think he may have finally moved on. He stopped texting and I didn't see him at Stumptown last night."

"I'm surprised you could see anything," Marcus laughed.

Justus sighed and looked at his friends. "Fine. Let's not talk about that again."

The three ate their lunch while continuing their playful bantering. When they finished, Marcus paid their bill. Scotty and Justus insisted on at least paying the tip, and both quickly pulled out a couple fives from their wallets.

When Justus glanced at the door, he noticed a man seated at the table by the front window. He was pleasant looking with dark hair, dark eyes, and a killer five-o'clock shadow. He could be Justus' type if he had not been staring at Scotty.

"Hey, Scotty," Justus whispered and leaned closer. "Don't look now, but that guy by the front window. He's staring at you."

"Where?" Scotty asked and turned his head to see.

"Not now!" Justus groaned. He looked at the man who had turned away. He obviously knew Justus had told his friend. "Never mind."

The three said their goodbyes on the sidewalk outside the café. Scotty declined Justus' offer of a ride home, saying he wanted to check out a new store downtown. Justus watched him walk away and turned to Marcus.

"Did you drive or would you like a lift home?" he asked.

"I drove, but can we go for a walk? There's something I'd like to talk to you about."

Justus glanced at his car across the street. "Sure, let me feed the meter first."

"Sure."

The two jaywalked. Justus purchased another parking pass from the kiosk and placed it on his dashboard, taking the old one away. Relocking the passenger door, he turned around to Marcus.

"Lead the way."

The two headed west to SW 12th Avenue. They crossed over to Jake's on the corner and turned south. They walked in silence for nearly the entire block before Marcus said anything.

"I have a huge favor to ask you."

"Sure, what?" Justus said without hesitation.

"I want you to be the executor of my will."

"What?" Justus stopped in the middle of Washington Street. Marcus grabbed his arm and pulled him the rest of the way to the sidewalk.

"It's no big deal," he said.

"We're too young to have wills. Those are for old people and people about to die." Justus' eyes widened as he looked at his friend. "You're not—"

"No," Marcus answered and smiled. "Since I now own a house, my accountant—"

"You have an accountant?" Justus' mouth dropped open.

"Yes. She files my taxes and stuff. She has been on me about having a will written up ever since I bought the house. I want you to be my executor."

"Sure, but why me?"

"You're my best friend. I trust you to take care of things."

Best friend, the words echoed in Justus' ears. "Okay, I'll do it but you have to promise me something."

"Okay, I promise."

"Wait, you don't know what I want you to promise. I want you to promise that you won't die for a long time."

Marcus laughed. "I promise."

The two continued their walk down 12th Street.

"Do you think we'll ever find Jack?"

"No," Marcus answered.

"Why?" Justus asked, trying not to sound shocked.

"I don't know. It's only a feeling. Jack is an attorney. He's not some flighty twink who runs off on a whim. He has responsibilities and people depending on him. He wouldn't up and disappear without a word. For the weekend maybe but not for this long."

"What do you suppose happened to him?"

"I don't know, but whatever it was, it's not good."

"Do you think he's dead?"

Marcus did not answer but his silence did. Justus looked

at the intersection ahead.

"Look at that old stone church," he said when they reached the intersection of SW Taylor Street. "That's the second one I've seen."

"And there's another church a couple blocks up. Haven't you seen them before?" Marcus asked.

"Yes," Justus admitted. "Only I never realized there were so many. We should head back."

They turned around. The walk back to their waiting cars seemed quicker. They stopped when they reached the Stark Street intersection.

"So, are you still coming out Monday night to Stumptown's Saint Paddy's Day Bash?" Marcus asked.

"Wouldn't miss it," Justus answered. They said their goodbyes and Justus watched Marcus cross the street to his waiting car parked outside of Jake's.

When Justus turned around and started for his car, he caught a glimpse of Dean's apartment building. A thought flashed in his mind. He wondered why he had not heard from Dean. Did he finally get the message?

On the drive back home, Justus turned the radio up until he felt the bass vibrate through the steering wheel. Still it was not loud enough to drown out the voices in his head that kept replaying his conversation with Marcus and his confusing feelings about Dean's silence. A feeling of dread and hopelessness began to pull at him.

Justus shut off the radio when he reached NE 62nd Avenue. Harrison hated hearing people's car radios blaring. He parked in front of the house and noticed Douglas' truck parked in the driveway behind Harrison's CR-V.

"So, how was lunch?" Harrison greeted him from the living room.

"Fine," Justus answered and closed the front door.

"That didn't sound fine," Douglas spoke up. He tilted his head back while he lay stretched out on the sofa.

Harrison paused the TV, freezing Shelly Winters underwater. "Come in here," he said to Justus. "What happened?"

Justus walked over to the empty chair between the TV and sofa. He sat down.

"It's really nothing. Marcus doesn't think we'll ever find Jack. I had the feeling he thinks Jack is dead."

Harrison's face registered shock. "Why?"

"He didn't say exactly. It was merely a feeling."

"Well, I wouldn't worry too much about it," Douglas said. "People have been found months, even years, after they have disappeared. He could have had a breakdown due to too much stress. He could have wanted to get away."

"You really think so?" Justus felt a flicker of hope inside.

"Why not?" Douglas answered. "Let the police do their job."

Justus slumped. The flicker of hope disappeared. "A lot of good that is. I still haven't heard from them."

"Give them time," Harrison said. "It's only been a week since you filed the report."

"But shouldn't they have found something by now?"

"Not always, but that doesn't mean they aren't working on it."

"I don't know," Justus said and stood up. "I think I'll go to my room."

"Okay." Harrison nodded.

"Hey," Douglas said and grabbed Justus' wrist as he passed. Justus looked at him. "It's going to be all right." He winked.

Justus smiled. "Oh, if you weren't Harry's, I'd be all over you," he teased.

Douglas let go of Justus and laughed.

"He's not mine and we're not gay," Harrison said firmly.

"Just kidding," Justus said while he headed up the stairs.

CHAPTER SIX

Monday morning arrived. Justus pulled his green shirt and green and gold plaid vest out of his closet. He put on a pair of denim blue skinny jeans. *Green jeans would be over doing it.* Before leaving his bedroom, he grabbed his green top hat.

After Harrison stopped laughing and they had finished their cup of coffee, they headed off to work. The drive was quiet except for Justus' nagging thoughts. He had been awakened in the middle of the night by an overwhelming feeling of fear. *What if Dean had disappeared like Jack and Alexander?* Justus looked out the passenger window at the passing scenery.

Harrison parked in the parking garage on SW 4th Avenue between Pine and Oak Streets instead of his usual garage. He told Justus it was so they could save some time and get home before the streets got crazy. Justus did not care. He would be part of that *crazy* when he came back into town for the party.

As luck had it, they had the elevator car to themselves. Justus watched the display above the buttons beside the door count off the floors.

"You're awfully quiet this morning," Harrison said while he leaned against the back wall. "Still worried about Dean?"

Justus looked at Harrison with a shocked expression. "How did you know?"

"Every Monday morning since you hooked up with him you've been on pins and needles when you've come to work."

"Yeah, well, I haven't heard from him in a week. I think he finally got the message."

"That's great!" Harrison said and playfully slapped Justus on the back.

Justus forced a smile but inside he was still confused by what he felt. Part of him was relieved, but another part was worried. He did not want anything to do with Dean, but at the same time, he did not want any harm to come to him either.

The elevator stopped. The doors opened and they stepped out onto the twenty-eighth floor.

"See you later," Harrison said when they reached the file room.

Justus watched him cross the floor to his office. He turned and looked at his desk in the middle of the file room. His heart sank a bit. His desk was exactly as he had left it on Friday, clear.

He took off his hat and set it on the corner of his desk. Sitting down, he opened the top drawer and flipped through a stack of CDs. Pulling out one, he popped it into his player and turned up the volume. The Weather Girls began singing their iconic gay anthem.

Justus picked up a stack of account files from his cart and began returning them to their proper cabinets. While the music played he felt his spirits lifting. He began dancing and singing along with the two women. When he filed the last account away, he grabbed his top hat and put it on. Throwing his head right and left, he sang and spun around with his hands over his head then came to an abrupt stop.

"Vicki!" he gasped and felt his face turning red. "How long have you been standing there?"

"Long enough," she answered with a laugh that jiggled her belly.

"Oh."

"Relax," she said with a wink, "I'm teasing. I just walked in."

Even though she told him to relax he could not stop from blushing. He noticed the large bouquet of green carnations and baby's breath in her hands. His breath caught.

"Are those for me?" he asked.

"Yes," she answered and set the vase down on his desk. "Your boyfriend caught me in the lobby again and gave them to me to give you. You're sure lucky to have a man like him. What's this, the third bouquet in less than a month?"

"He's not my boyfriend," Justus said in a terse tone that caused Vicki to step back.

"I'm sorry," she said, sounding a bit surprised. "If a man sent me flowers as often as this guy does, I'd make him my boyfriend. There aren't many like him out there."

Listening to Vicki ramble on only made Justus' anxiety worse. He was glad Dean had not disappeared like Jack and the other guy, but at the same time he remembered the look that had been in Dean's eyes and his tight grip on his arm. It scared him.

"What's wrong?" Vicki asked. "You look miles away."

"Nothing," Justus answered and shuddered.

"Do you want me to take them away?" Vicki asked.

"No, they're fine."

Justus could not help but see the disappointment in Vicki's eyes as she turned away.

"On second thought, take them."

Vicki turned back. "No, you should keep them. They go with your outfit." She smiled. "I've got to get back to work. See ya'." She left before Justus could insist she take the flowers. Now he felt sorry for her.

He looked at the bouquet again and noticed the card. He grabbed it and tore it open. Pulling out the card, he skipped the printed message and went straight to Dean's inscription.

Happy St. Paddy's Day. Sorry I wasn't in touch last week. I had to go to Bend. I had some personal issues I needed to deal with. Hope you didn't miss me too much. Have a great day. Love, Dean.

Justus set the card on his desk and looked at the flowers again. No matter how nice the card and flowers were, there was still something about the man that left him confused. He grabbed his push cart and headed straight for Harrison's office.

Harrison was on his telephone with his back toward the doorway. Justus left his cart outside and walked over to Harrison's desk. He sat down on the corner and waited for Harrison to finish.

"I told you I have no idea where she went," Harrison snapped at the phone. "Well, believe what you want. You always do anyway."

While Justus listened, his thoughts about Dean faded away. Instead he wondered who Harrison could be talking to. *Surely it wasn't a client.*

"I don't care. You brought this on yourself.—What did you expect? Be thankful it was her because I would have stomped your miserable ass into the ground first!—Don't even go there with me. I may be clear across the country but I'm not stupid." Harrison's voice began to rise which made Justus a bit nervous. He had never seen this side of Harrison. "This conversation is over. I've got work to do, and don't call me at this number again!" Harrison spun his chair around and slammed the receiver down on the cradle so hard Justus thought he would break it. Harrison jumped and let out a yell when he saw Justus.

"What are you doing?" he snapped when he recovered from the shock.

"Waiting to talk to you," Justus answered and tried to stifle his laughter.

"What about?" Harrison asked and rolled his chair up to his desk. "Get off," he said and smacked Justus' thigh lightly with the back of his hand.

Justus did not move.

"Who was that on the phone?" he asked.

"My stupid brother-in-law," Harrison answered, sounding disgusted.

"Oh."

"He insists I know where Dani and the boys are, but I don't!" he said, raising his voice and directing his words at his telephone.

"So, what's he going to do now?"

"I have no idea. He's pretty angry."

"You'll have to warn Dani when she finally contacts you."

"I know," Harrison answered. "So, what do you want?" he asked and looked at Justus.

"I forgot."

"Well, get off my desk." Again, Harrison slapped at the side of Justus' leg.

Justus hopped down. "Oh!" he gasped and turned back toward Harrison. "Dean's okay. He was in Bend last week."

Harrison looked confused. "Okay, and we are happy

because?"

"Just sayin'," Justus answered and shrugged his shoulders indifferently. He headed back to the file room.

Justus tossed the card and envelope into the trash can under his desk and took the flowers down to Vicki. She was not at her desk so he left them for her.

Returning to his file room, he piled everything from his desk onto his chair. Once it was full, he wheeled it around to Debra's old desk and unloaded it. After the switch was finished, he sat down and surveyed his new view. Instead of facing the wall, he now faced the doorway and could see whoever entered before they had the chance to startle him. He plugged in his CD player and pressed the power button. Instantly the CD began playing where it had left off.

The rest of the morning passed quickly. Justus made his morning rounds, collecting files that needed to go back to the file room. He turned up his music and began putting the files away when he noticed Harrison standing in his doorway.

"Oh, hi," Justus said and turned his CD player down a touch.

"Nice to see you're back to your old self," Harrison said. "What on earth are you listening to?"

"A CD of eighties dance music. Marcus made it for me."

Harrison shook his head and laughed. "You have a call on *my* phone."

"I do?" Justus said and looked panicked.

"No, it's not him. It's the police," Harrison said to calm his fears.

"Oh," Justus sighed with relief. "I gave the police your number. I figured you're always at your desk so it would be the best number for them to reach me. I knew you wouldn't mind." He smiled and gave Harrison a wink.

Harrison gave him a what-am-I-going-to-do-with-you sort of look.

"Did they sound like they had good news?" Justus asked while the two headed back to Harrison's cubicle.

"I don't know. The woman asked for you and I said I would go get you," Harrison answered.

"I wonder if they found Jack," Justus said when they reached Harrison's desk. "Which line?"

"Here." Harrison handed Justus the receiver, tapped his phone and then nodded to Justus.

"Hi, this is Justus," he said while he sat down on his corner of Harrison's desk.

"Mr. Reynolds, I'm Detective Kennedy with the Portland Police. I've been looking into the disappearance of Mr. O'Brien."

"Yes," Justus said, holding the receiver a little tighter, his heart beating a bit faster. He smiled at Harrison.

"I regret to inform you that—"

Justus listened and felt a sinking sensation in his chest. The smile on his face faded away. His shoulders slumped. He stopped wiggling his feet.

"Okay. Well, thank you for letting me know." Justus leaned over and returned the receiver to its cradle.

"So?" Harrison asked while he sat leaning back in his chair. "What did she say? Did they find your friend?"

"No. They haven't found him," Justus answered. His shoulders slumped. He stared at the floor.

"Give them time, they'll—"

"The police lady said they talked with everyone they could find at Stumptown and at his apartment building and haven't come up with any leads. Since he's an adult and he doesn't have any known medical issues, they are suspending their investigation. She did say they'll keep it open, but they won't actively be working on it."

"I'm so sorry, Justus," Harrison said and rocked forward. "I wish I knew what else to say."

"That's okay," Justus said, sounding defeated. "I guess I'll have to tell the others." He started to reach for Harrison's phone but Harrison grabbed it.

"You can do that from your own phone," he said.

"Fine," Justus snapped.

"Or you could wait to tell them in person tonight. There's no rush is there?"

"I guess not. You know," he said while he stood up, "you should come out and have a drink with us one of these nights."

Harrison raised an eyebrow. "I don't think so. That's not my scene," he said and shook his head.

"Not my what?" Justus laughed. "Harry, no one says that anymore. You really need to keep up." He laughed again. "Not my scene," he repeated in a mock deep voice.

"Alright, get back to work."

Heading back to the file room, Justus felt his spirits gradually lift. The dread he felt after the brief conversation with the police officer slowly faded. He decided to take Harrison's advice and wait until the gang met up in a few hours to tell them.

CHAPTER SEVEN

Justus parked his car on SW 12th Avenue in front of the Presbyterian Church. He laughed to himself when he thought of the irony of it. The pastor of the church had opposed having a gay club go in less than a block away. He had argued they would take parking away from his parishioners. The owner of CC's Nightclub countered with the argument that most of their clientele would be parking after normal business hours and not during the day, when the church would be having its services. The city planners agreed and CC's was approved.

Normally Justus would have parked in his usual spot across from O'Bryant Square on SW 9th Avenue, but with the holiday and party, all the spaces filled up early. He locked the doors of his car and headed for Stumptown five blocks away.

A small cluster of people had gathered on the corner of SW 12th and Washington. A couple were dressed in drag, and Justus recognized them from posters that hung on the wall outside the restrooms at Stumptown. They were performers at

Embers, a drag nightclub on the corner of Broadway and Burnside. According to the poster, the red-wigged queen was Miss Scarlett and the shorter, dark-haired queen was Cherry Royale.

While Justus waited for the walk light to change, he overheard bits of their conversation. It sounded as though the queens were trying to console one of the men.

"It's going to be okay," Miss Scarlett said in a slightly falsetto voice. She had an arm around a shorter man who was dressed in jeans and a plaid shirt. The man kept his head down.

"He doesn't answer his phone and his neighbors said they haven't seen him in a week." His voice sounded strained.

"Excuse me, but who are you talking about?" Justus interrupted.

Cherry Royale's back straightened. She turned and looked him up and down with a disdainful expression.

"No one you know, sweetie," she said in a condescending but very manly voice. "So why don't you mind your own business and beat it."

Justus felt his face turn red. The light changed and he started to walk across the street ahead of them.

"Cherry!" Miss Scarlett snapped. "That was rude, even for you. Hey, kid," she called to Justus. He stopped and turned around. "We were talking about another friend of ours who disappeared. No one has seen him."

"I think I heard about him. Alexander?"

"Yes, he's the one," Miss Scarlett answered and looked puzzled.

"My friend Marcus told me about him," Justus explained.

"Marcus Morelli?" one of the men asked in a surprised tone.

"Yes, you know him?" Justus answered and looked at the

fourth man. He was husky and dark haired with a thick mustache and eyebrows. Not at all what Justus knew as Marcus' type.

"I do," he answered. "Tell him, Curtis says hi."

"Okay," Justus responded while he tried to focus back to their conversation. He looked back at Miss Scarlett. "I'm sorry."

"We were talking about another friend, Cody," she continued. The group stopped when they reached the other side of the street and huddled on the corner to talk.

"Cody?" Justus repeated. He had not heard of him.

"The last time I saw him," the man beside Miss Scarlett spoke, "was at their CC's Mardi Gras party last Tuesday. He had been drinking a lot and working the crowd. Right before midnight he came up to me with some Hollywood-looking guy. He was all happy and excited. He whispered in my ear that the guy had been buying him drinks all night and was loaded. He said he thought he found his prince. I told him he was drunk and he wasn't thinking clearly. He got all upset with me and left with the guy anyway. That was it, the last time I saw him."

"It's going to be okay, Patrick," Miss Scarlett said and hugged him while he dried his eyes.

"Did you get the guy's name?" Justus asked.

Patrick shook his head.

"What did he look like?" Justus asked feeling his heart begin to race. This was the first person who actually saw the man and could identify him.

"I don't remember, exactly."

"Come on, think!" Justus insisted.

"Hey! Hey!" Cherry Royale barked and stepped between Justus and Patrick. "He doesn't remember. Leave him alone."

"I'm sorry. A friend of mine, Jack, is missing too. He disappeared at the Stumptown's Valentine's Day party. No one knows anything and the police stopped looking—"

"That figures," Cherry Royale quipped. "They're only worried if some old *straight* guy with Alzheimer's goes missing. They don't care about people like us."

"That's a bit of exaggeration, Cherry," Miss Scarlett said, but her expression seemed to say she agreed with Cherry.

"Whatever," Cherry Royale said, brushing her off. "It's true. Watch the news and see for yourself. They won't even put his or Alexander's disappearance on the news, but they'll report on the mayor's missing dog."

"That's true," Curtis agreed and nodded. "I saw that."

"Has anyone tried?" Justus asked. "I mean, calling the news."

"I called the local station," Curtis answered. "They said it wasn't exciting enough or something like that."

"Have you had any success with your friend?" Miss Scarlett asked and looked at Justus.

"I've only talked to the police and they couldn't find any leads."

"Well, maybe with three of us missing they might think it's newsworthy," she speculated.

"Possibly," Justus answered.

"Hey, look at the time!" Cherry Royale said, holding up her arm and pointing at a man's heavy wristwatch. "You've got forty-five minutes until your show. We better get going. See ya, kid."

"I hope you find your friend," Miss Scarlett said with a smile.

Justus watched the two queens rush off down the street, past CC's, toward Burnside.

"You headed for CC's?" Curtis asked while they walked along the sidewalk toward Stark Street. He stopped when they reached CC's and opened the door. Loud country-western music poured out.

"No, I'm headed to Stumptown," Justus answered and nodded toward Stark Street.

"Okay," Curtis answered. "See ya'." Patrick went into the club without speaking. Curtis followed letting the door close behind him.

Justus picked up his step. His mind whirled with the new information. *Three people have disappeared but now there was a clue. The man was dark haired, a Hollywood type. Loaded and buying people drinks. Surely the police will do something now.*

Stumptown's Saint Paddy's day bash was only for those who had prepurchased tickets, and a crowd of disappointed club-hoppers were gathered around the entrance. Justus felt the pocket of his shirt and found his. He showed it to the doorman and went inside.

Strings of green lights were draped above the bar. Cardboard cutouts of green-glittered shamrocks dangled from the ceiling on thin black threads. The DJ was dressed in a leprechaun costume complete with red wig and beard and green, buckled top hat. Justus grabbed a rum and Coke from the bar and headed across the dance floor to meet up with his friends.

"Isn't this nuts!" Dale said while he stood dancing in place at their table. "Tons of new faces and hot men everywhere."

"Yeah, it's great," Scotty said, sounding impressed but not as overjoyed as Dale.

Justus sat down beside Scotty.

"Where's Marcus?" he asked.

Scotty motioned with his head toward the dance floor. Marcus was dancing with a shirtless man who had painted his chest green.

"Oh," Justus answered. "Have you guys been here long?"

Scotty looked at his watch. "About a half an hour. We got here at eight thirty so we could grab a table. What took you so long?"

"I had to park on 12th, five blocks away."

"Oh," Scotty said and nodded.

A server appeared and took their order. Justus ordered their St. Paddy's special, a green fruity drink in a large, round glass. Dale went for a mug of green beer and Scotty ordered a Coke. Marcus returned to the table right in time and ordered his drink.

Justus waited for the server to leave before he leaned toward the center of the table so he would not have to shout.

"Have I got news for you," he started. "I heard from the police today."

"You did?" Dale said, sounding anxious and shocked.

Justus looked at him and frowned, letting him know it was not good news. "A policewoman called to inform me they talked to the landlord and the bartenders at Stumptown, but no one saw anything. She said, since they don't have any fresh leads and he's a healthy adult, they're suspending the search."

"What?" Dale shouted in anger and disbelief.

"She said they'll keep the file open in case something comes up." Justus quickly added in an attempt to calm Dale.

"Oh great!" Dale grumbled.

"Well, maybe if we tell them about Alexander, they might—"

"They already know about him," Justus interrupted Scotty. "However, I ran into Miss Scarlett from Embers and she said that another man is missing, a guy named Cody."

Everyone looked shocked.

"When?" Marcus asked.

"Last Tuesday night at CC's Mardi Gras party," Justus

answered. "By the way, Curtis says hi."

Marcus smiled but appeared unfazed. "Did anyone see anything?"

"As a matter of fact, someone did. Cody's friend Patrick saw the guy."

"Really?" Dale sat forward in his chair.

"Yeah, but when I asked him what the guy looked like, he claims not to remember other than he was rich and was a *Hollywood-looking* guy."

"Oh great! What's that supposed to mean?" Dale groused and sat back, obviously disgusted.

"Well, with what we already know, he's dark haired, handsome, and rich. He buys guys drinks," Justus said.

"Oh, that's good!" Dale remarked in a sarcastic tone. "I bet he even had two arms, two legs and a penis."

"Not funny," Justus snapped at him.

"Well, look around. Nearly every guy in here fits that description. How are we to figure out which one he is, *if* he's even here?"

"Did they tell the police?" Marcus asked changing the subject.

"It didn't sound like it. By the way Cherry Royale was talking, I doubt they will."

"Why? What did she say?" Marcus asked.

"She thinks that the police and media won't do anything for guys like us."

"Well, she's right," Dale grumbled.

The server returned with their drinks. They all paid him and he headed away to the next table.

"So, now what do we do?" Scotty asked.

"What can we do? If the police can't find him, how are we supposed to?" Marcus answered.

"I don't know. We have to keep our eyes open."

"Brilliant idea," Dale said and took a big swig of his beer.

The conversation stalled. Marcus turned away to look at another green man on the dance floor.

Justus looked around the nightclub. The men were packed in so tight that it was standing room only.

"Has anyone seen Dean?" he spoke up.

"I haven't seen him," Scotty answered.

"How should I know?" Dale sulked and continued to empty his beer mug.

"Well, if it helps, I haven't seen your guy," Marcus answered.

"He's not my guy," Justus insisted.

"You know what I mean," Marcus said.

"So, how was your—" Justus was interrupted by the server, dressed in a green vest without a shirt underneath, setting a napkin in front of Scotty and then a colorful drink in a large wine glass.

"What's this?" Scotty asked and gave the man a confused look.

"It's a Layered Lemon Drop. It's tinted green instead of yellow because of it being Saint Paddy's Day."

"But I didn't order this."

"I know," the server answered. "It's from that man at the end of the bar." He waved and the man who bought the drink waved back.

Everyone turned to look. Justus felt his body go numb while Patrick's words rushed back at him like a tsunami.

"Not bad," Marcus said and raised his eyebrows. "I wouldn't exactly call him a Hollywood type, but. . ."

"Does this have alcohol in it?" Scotty asked the server.

"This is a bar," he answered in a duh sort of tone. "Yes."

"Oh," Scotty said and looked at the drink again. "Well, take it back, I don't want it."

The server looked surprised. "I can't take it back. It's already paid for."

"Can I get another?" Marcus interrupted and held up his empty glass.

"Sure. You?"

"I'll have another special," Justus answered.

"What about you?" The server looked at Dale.

"I'll have another green beer."

"I'll be right back." The server slipped away.

"Scotty, don't drink that," Justus warned.

"I wasn't going to."

"Oh great, the guy's still looking over here," Dale spoke up. "Scotty, pretend to take a sip. He's watching you."

"I don't care." Scotty pushed the drink away.

"Scott, it would be rude to not at least go thank the man," Dale said, eyeing the man across the club. "Who knows, he might be your Mister Right."

"He might also be the kidnapper."

"Kids are napped. Adults are abducted," Dale corrected.

"Whatever," Justus snipped. He glanced at Marcus who was suddenly very silent. Marcus sat staring at the drink. Justus could not tell what his friend was thinking.

"Fine," Scotty snapped, sounding angry. He stood up and picked up the drink and napkin.

"Scotty," Marcus said and grabbed Scotty's arm. The two looked at each other. "Be careful."

Scotty looked across the room and his angry expression faded to a more worried look. He looked back at Marcus and nodded. "I will."

The three watched while Scotty wove his way through

the crowd.

"You don't think he'll throw it on him, do you?" Justus asked.

"No," Marcus insisted. "Scotty's too nice a guy to do something like that."

They watched while Scotty approached the dark-haired man at the end of the bar.

"Wish I could hear what Scott's saying," Marcus said.

"Well, judging from the man's expression, it must not be too bad," Justus observed.

"You know, from here he's really not bad looking," Dale said, still eyeing the drink benefactor. "Looks like he has a nice body. I'd do him."

"Well, I'm outta here," Marcus said and stood up. He disappeared into the crowd before either Dale or Justus could say a word.

"What's with him?" Dale asked a bit confused.

"I don't know," Justus answered, keeping what he thought to himself.

"I don't believe it!"

"It's true," Justus said in his defense. "I don't."

"No, not that. Look, Scotty actually took a drink of that thing," Dale answered.

"You've got to be kidding." Justus looked across the room at Scotty and the mystery man.

"Here we go," the server said and set the two drinks down on the table in front of Justus and Dale. "Where's your other friend?"

"He's around," Justus answered. "I'll cover his drink." He gave the money to the server who then set the fruity drink on the table.

Dale handed his money over plus an extra nice tip.

"Thanks," the server said. "My name's Lex."

"I'm Dale and this is Justus."

"Pleased," Lex said and eyed them. "Are you two a couple?"

"Oh, hell no," Dale answered.

"Thanks a lot," Justus quipped, sounding offended.

"We're just friends," Dale added.

Lex's smile widened. "Well, if you need anything, don't hesitate to ask."

"Sure," Dale said.

"Oh great, now I suppose you're going to go off and do him and leave me here alone with Scotty?"

"Hey, you took off the other night," Dale reminded him. He looked over to the bar and then started looking around the club. "They're gone!"

"Who's gone?" Justus asked and looked at the bar.

"Scotty and that man," Dale answered. "And Marcus and green boy."

"Are you sure?" Justus stood up and looked around. His pulse quickened while a feeling of panic began to grow stronger.

"Yes, I'm sure," Dale answered.

"Oh no."

"He'll be okay. It's I'm-saving-myself-for-marriage Scotty, remember?" Dale said and laughed.

"Oh, knock it off," Justus snapped angrily. "That's not funny."

"Whatever," Dale mocked. He took a drink of his green beer and burped loudly.

"Gross!"

As the night wore on, Justus found himself alone at the table, growing more and more worried. Dale had gone off with Lex, and they were probably tucked away in that little room doing all sorts of things to each other. Justus shook the mental image from his head. Marcus had left a long time ago with green boy. Justus looked at his phone and the list of text messages he had been sending to Scotty. All were unanswered. He looked at the door for the millionth time.

He raised his glass to take another drink and realized it was empty. He glanced at his watch, almost time for last call. Looking back at the crowd, he felt a jolt radiate through his body starting at his chest and ending at his feet. He set his empty drink glass on the table and leaned back behind a nearby pillar.

Peeking out, he looked at the bar. Dean was talking to Barry. They appeared to be having a bit of an argument, but in the strobing dance-floor lights that separated Justus and the men, Justus could not be sure.

While keeping his eyes on the pair, Justus stood up and worked his way over to the door to make his escape before Dean spotted him. He pushed the heavy door open and immediately came face-to-face with the generous drink buyer. Both men jumped and the buyer took a step back. Justus took a quick look around.

"Hey, where's my friend?"

The dark-haired man looked confused. Now that he was in better lighting, Justus noticed that the man had a neatly trimmed mustache. "Friend?"

"The guy with the red hair you left here with two hours ago."

"That little tease?" The man laughed but was definitely not happy. "He took off, probably walked home or. . . I don't know."

"Where did you take him?"

"Who are you, his mother?" the man snapped.

If Justus had not moved out of the way, he was sure the

man would have knocked him aside. Justus watched the door close.

Remembering Dean was inside and could come out any second, Justus rushed back to his car. Safely inside with the doors locked, he took out his cell phone and began typing.

Where r u?

He waited. The screen on his phone timed out and went dark. Suddenly it vibrated and began to ring in his hand. Justus recognized the number and quickly answered it.

"Where are you?" he asked.

"I don't know. It's dark and my battery's going dead. I had to use it as a flashlight."

"What street are you on?"

"Let me check. I'm coming to a fork in the road."

Justus could hear gravel crunching under Scotty's feet while he walked.

"I think it says Remington and Cardinal?"

"Are you sure it's not Rivington and Cardinell?" Justus asked.

"It says R-I-V-I-N-G-T-O-N," Scotty spelled it out. "Yeah, Rivington."

"Okay, I'll be there shortly. Stay where you are."

"Hurry," Scotty said before the call disconnected.

Justus could hear the fear in Scotty's voice. He pulled away from the curb and headed for the West Hills.

Getting to where Scotty was waiting was a challenge due to the one-way streets and the road construction detours. Justus turned west on Washington and took a left onto SW 13th Avenue. Construction between Clay and Market Streets forced him to detour east on Columbia, taking him away from where Scotty was waiting. After going in circles around the Old Church and McMenamins Market Street Pub, Justus remembered another route. He headed east on Market Street and turned south on Broadway.

"Hang on Scotty, I'm coming," he said to himself.

In his hurry, he turned onto Clifton only to come to a dead end. Backing up in the dark, on such a narrow street was slow and tedious. Finally, Justus was back on Broadway heading south again. The road wound through the West Hills of Portland in a maze of dead-end side streets. Justus began to get worried he was getting lost when he saw a familiar street sign. He turned right onto Davenport and then a left onto SW 16th Avenue.

"I'm almost there, Scotty," he said aloud.

SW 16th cut a straight line down the hill toward Portland. Justus had almost come to the end of the road when he spotted the sign SW Cardinell Dr. He turned right onto an even narrower street that forced him to drive at what felt like a snail's pace. With his headlights on high beam, he wound his way deeper and deeper into the hillside neighborhood. After a tight turn that cast his headlights across the homes that sat at the edge of the street, he came to a wide intersection and stopped. He resisted the urge to honk his horn, due to the house that sat inches away from the bend in the road. Instead he pulled out his cell phone and speed dialed Scotty's number.

"Justus?" Scotty answered.

"I'm here. Where are you?"

"I see you. I'll—" Again the call was cut off.

Justus looked around in the darkness. If it were not for the porchlight on the house and his headlights, the intersection would have been pitch-black. A movement on the hillside ahead caught his attention. Scotty emerged from the undergrowth and trees. He ran to the car and opened the passenger door.

"Thank God you're here," he said, shutting the door once he was safely inside.

"What happened?"

"Get me out of here."

Justus turned left and headed down the hill. They wound their way along the narrow street making sharp turns left and right until they came to SW 12th Avenue and the road flattened out again.

"Where do you want to go?" Justus said, when they came to a stop light.

"Can I stay at your place tonight?" Scotty asked.

Justus remembered Harrison's rule, no overnight guests, but Scotty was not that type of guest. Surely Harrison would not mind Scotty spending the night, especially after his ordeal.

"Sure," Justus answered.

They stopped by Scotty's apartment. Justus waited in the car while Scotty went inside and grabbed a change of clothes and his toothbrush. Once he was back in the car they headed for Harrison's.

"Are you okay?" Justus asked him once they crossed the Burnside Bridge.

"I will be."

"What happened? I mean, when I left Stumptown I ran into that guy—"

"Andy?"

"Is that his name?" Scotty nodded and Justus continued, "I asked him where you were and he said some rather rude stuff."

"He's a psycho," Scotty said. "He said he wanted to go someplace where we could talk without all the commotion. I thought he meant Shari's or Denny's or some café but he took me to his house on, how did you pronounce that name, Revington?"

"Riv-ing-ton," Justus answered.

"Yeah, well," Scotty said and continued. "I must admit, I was pretty nervous but up to that point he seemed okay, even a bit nervous like me. We talked about what we do for work."

"You didn't tell him where you work, did you?" Justus interrupted.

"No. I remember your rules. We simply talked in general. He said he works for his family's business. Judging by his house it must be a successful business. It's really nice. It overlooks some trees and, in the distance, you can see the lights of downtown. It did have a strange smell though. I almost threw up."

"That bad, eh?"

"Yeah. I can't describe it exactly, but after a while I didn't notice it anymore.

"He offered me a drink and I turned him down. Then he sat down on the couch next to me and tried to start something. I told him he was moving too fast and that's when things got really strange."

"How so?"

"He got mad. He started complaining how all he ever does is be nice to people and helps people and whenever he needs anything, everyone turns away. I was beginning to think I may have found that Dean guy's double.

"When I said perhaps I should leave, he really lost it. He practically shoved me out the door and told me I could walk back to town. Honestly, Justus, I was terrified. I wasn't sure what he was going to do."

"Well, you're safe now," Justus said and put his hand on Scotty's knee to reassure him.

CHAPTER EIGHT

Justus moved to the back of the elevator beside Harrison to make room for the rest of the passengers. The doors slid shut, and the car began to rise. Justus watched the lighted display count the floors.

"How's Scotty?" Harrison asked. It had been four days since the ordeal.

"He's okay," Justus answered, though, deep down, he was not as sure. In the year plus since he had met Scotty, he had never known him to leave the club with anyone, especially since he was not the type to hook up. He wondered what had prompted him to do it at the party.

The elevator stopped and the doors opened. Justus waited until the people in front of him either stepped aside or walked out before he followed Harrison.

"I am worried about him, though," Justus told Harrison once they were no longer in a tight crowd.

"I know," Harrison agreed. "I must admit, I was a bit

surprised myself. Scotty's a nice guy. I didn't think he was like the rest of you."

"What!" Justus gasped in mock offense.

"I only meant he seems quiet and reserved."

"Uh-huh, nice try," Justus said and pursed his lips to keep from laughing.

While they headed to the office, Harrison continued to try to dig himself out of the hole he had dug. Justus reveled at seeing Harrison squirm and get all red-faced. He knew what Harrison had meant but he was not about to let him off the hook just yet.

When they reached the file room, Justus decided it had been long enough.

"I know what you meant and it's okay. You're right. Scotty isn't the type to have casual sex," Justus said, lowering his voice. "There's something else I wanted to tell you. I saw Dean Monday night. I didn't speak to him and I don't think he saw me, but I saw him. He was talking to that Barry guy I told you about."

"Good. Maybe he's moved on."

"I don't know about that. It didn't appear like they were having that type of conversation. In fact, Dean looked pretty intense, like he did when he grabbed my arm."

"Oh, I see. What did you do?" Harrison asked.

"I got the hell out of there."

"He didn't see you?"

"I don't think so," Justus answered.

"Good. You have nothing to worry about then. See ya' later."

Justus turned to go into the file room and froze. "Harry!" he called but was careful not to shout.

Harrison stopped. "What?" he asked and walked back to

Justus.

"He's not letting up!" Justus said and nodded into the room.

"Oh my!" Harrison responded when he saw the vase with a red rose sitting on the empty desk.

"Take it away," Justus ordered.

"Maybe it's not from him," Harrison suggested, but his tone said differently.

"It's from him, I know it," Justus insisted. "No one else would send me flowers."

"Look, there's a card. Read it before you jump to conclusions."

"Fine," Justus said. He hated it when Harrison used words that reminded him of his father. Growing up Justus' father had always been telling him not to jump to conclusions, insinuating he was wrong. Hearing those words felt like a put down. He hated that feeling.

Harrison picked up the white envelope and vase. He handed the envelope to Justus and waited.

Justus' hands shook while he tore the flap open. He glanced at Harrison while he pulled the flat card out. Looking at it he was confused. He flipped it over to the back and then the front.

"That's odd," he said and held it out for Harrison to see. "It's blank."

"That is odd," Harrison agreed. "Still want me to take this away?"

"I guess not. Maybe I was wrong."

Harrison handed the vase to Justus and left.

Slowly Justus walked into the file room and set the vase down on the empty desk.

"I see you got my flower."

Justus spun around and let out a muffled yell, pressing his hands over his mouth. He fell back and half-sat, half-leaned against the top of the desk.

"What are you doing in here?" he said when his surprise was replaced with anger.

"I wanted to see you again," Dean answered and took a step into the room.

"How did you find me?"

"I gave that woman the flower and then followed her up here," Dean explained and looked around the room. "What a dreadful office. You can't even see outside."

"I like it. Besides, I don't spend a lot of time in here," Justus said. "What do you want?"

"I already told you, I only wanted to see you and to let you know that Barry—that is his name, isn't it?"

"What about him?"

"He won't be bothering you anymore."

"He never bothered me," Justus said.

"Well, that's good," Dean said and smiled. It was not a smile that put Justus at ease. It was a creepy sort of smile, almost sinister and evil. "Will you be going out tonight?"

"I don't know."

"Come on, I know you always go out on Friday nights. Don't lie to me."

The tone in Dean's voice hinted at anger which made Justus' heart pound and his fear rise.

"I'll see you tonight," Dean said firmly. He turned around and left.

Justus' knees gave out the moment Dean was out of sight. He fell into the office chair beside him. His whole body trembled.

"Was that—"

Justus jumped and nearly slid out of the chair. He looked up and saw Harrison standing in the doorway.

"Oh my god, are you okay?" Harrison asked and rushed to Justus' side.

"Yes, it was Dean."

"How did he—" Harrison grabbed the telephone receiver. "Never mind, I'm calling security."

"No, don't," Justus said and stopped him. "Let him go."

"Well, then we should call the police."

"No," Justus answered and shook his head. "Cherry Royale was right. The cops around here don't care about guys like us. They won't do anything. They'd probably just laugh."

"So what do you want to do?"

"Nothing."

"Nothing? But he—"

"I'm okay," Justus answered and started to stand up but his legs felt weak and unsteady. He fell back down onto the chair.

Harrison gave Justus a look that reminded him of his father. It was a look that his father gave whenever he knew Justus was not telling the truth.

"I'll be fine in a minute. Please take that flower out of here."

Harrison seemed to hesitate for a moment but finally picked up the vase. "Okay," he said. "If you need me, I'll be at my desk."

Justus watched him leave and with him, the flower. He sat back in the chair and took several deep breaths before trying to stand up again. He walked around to his desk and sat down again. He reached for the telephone to call Scotty but realized it was too early. Scotty did not start work until nine. Instead, he switched his CD player on. Instantly the room was filled with the sound of Anita Ward's voice belting out a '70s disco song that sounded like an old telephone company ad. He closed his eyes for a moment and let the music erase his stress.

Time seemed to slip away unnoticed. Justus busied himself refiling stacks of account folders and logging them into his computer system. It was not until Harrison stuck his head in the doorway and told him it was time for lunch that he realized he was hungry.

The two crowded into the elevator and headed down to the main floor, to the small café in the indoor courtyard. Ever since Justus started working with Harrison, the two of them had lunch together. Always at the same little café and always the same thing: chicken rice bowl, no veggie, light sauce, and a large Coke. Justus never tired of the food or desired to change it up. He liked it. It tasted good. Plus, most days he was able to get Harrison to pay for it.

He snagged a table by the window of a boutique store that sold incense, candles, and perfumed oils. One of the employees was taking down the Saint Patrick's Day decorations and hanging up paper bunny rabbits with baskets and mesh eggs of various sizes and colors. He waved at the young man who smiled back.

Harrison returned carrying a tray with two plastic bowls and two large cups of Coke. He set the tray on the table.

"Friend of yours?" he asked.

"I saw him at the club once and no, we didn't hook up," Justus quickly added.

"I never said you did," Harrison said, sounding a bit defensive. He pulled out a chair across from Justus and sat down with his back to the window. "Speaking of the club, are you still planning going out tonight?"

"Yes," Justus answered.

"Do you think that's a good idea? I mean, what about Dean? Isn't he going to be there?"

"Probably, but I'm gonna see if I can talk the guys into going to CC's instead."

"That would probably be a good idea." Harrison nodded. He took a drink of his Coke.

Justus looked at Harrison and a smile spread slowly across his lips. "You have no idea what CC's is, do you?"

Harrison looked up at Justus. He shook his head. "No, not really."

"It's a country-western club on 12th across from the Presbyterian Church. It's not as busy as Stumptown and the music isn't my taste, but we can still have a fun time."

"I see," Harrison answered. "So, have you talked to any of them yet?"

"I tried calling Scotty, but he didn't answer. He's probably busy. I can't call Dale at work. One day you'll have to meet his boss. He's really hot. He has a long—"

"Okay, eating here," Harrison interrupted. He held up his fork covered in rice and teriyaki sauce.

"I wasn't going to say anything bad. His boss has a long list of rules for everyone and one of his rules is no personal phone calls, texting, or emailing. What did you think I was going to say?" Justus grinned when he noticed Harrison was blushing.

"Never mind. So, what about your friend Mark?"

"You mean Marcus?" Justus corrected. "I haven't been able to reach him. He's not answering at home or at work."

"Have any of the guys talked to him?" Harrison asked.

"I don't know, I haven't asked. I'll see him tonight," Justus answered. "So, change of subject, have you heard from Dani yet?"

"No." Harrison sat back in his chair. "I got an email from Robert though. He still insists that I know where she is and has threatened to have my phone records subpoenaed."

"Can he do that?"

"I don't really know," Harrison answered. "But, then again, I don't really care. Let's eat."

Justus knew Harrison too well. He knew even though Harrison claimed otherwise that he was worried, worried about Dani and about what her husband would do. He took a sip of his Coke and continued to eat his lunch.

CHAPTER NINE

For the second time that week, Justus parked his car in front of the Presbyterian Church on SW 12th Avenue. It was not hard to get Scotty to agree to change venues for their Friday night get-together after his ordeal the previous Monday, but convincing Dale took some doing. After that, Justus sent a text to Marcus.

When Justus opened the solid wooden door to the nightclub, he was immediately struck by the twang of some country-western singer bemoaning the loss of a love or his broken-down pickup, Justus was not sure. This was not his favorite music. He walked up to the bar and, after showing his ID to the bartender, ordered a rum and Coke.

While he waited for his drink he looked around. CC's décor was rustic like Stumptown's but featured pub tables made of small wagon wheels topped with round glass. Saddles were hung on the wooden fence that separated a small dance floor from the sitting areas on both sides. Modified kerosene lanterns with amber lightbulbs hung from large nails hammered into the sides of the decorative wooden support pillars. As tacky as it was, it was a welcome change for Justus considering what he had been through that morning.

The bartender set a rum and Coke down on the bar and quickly made change for Justus' twenty. Justus stuffed the change into his pocket and picked up his drink. He looked around the club for his friends and spotted them across the room.

Marcus was seated beside Scotty and the two were talking. Dale sat across from them with a sour look on his face.

"Hi guys," Justus greeted. He pulled out the empty chair next to Dale and sat down.

"I still don't see why we had to change and come here for our night out?" Dale grumbled.

"I explained it to you on the phone," Justus answered, not in the mood to go over it again.

"Yeah, well, shouldn't we have voted on it or something?" Dale continued.

"No one is forcing you to come here. Justus is being stalked by a crazy man," Scotty answered in Justus' defense.

"What?" Marcus gasped.

"It's a long story, but what Scotty said is true," Justus admitted and then gave them a quick, abbreviated version of what had gone down that morning. "Dean has been sending me flowers and today even showed up where I work."

"If he's bothering you, why don't you go to the police?" Marcus asked.

"A lot of good that would do. They can't even find Jack or the other two missing guys. They won't do anything."

"True," Dale agreed. "So, speaking of Jack, what are we going to do? How are we going to find him?"

"What can we do?" Marcus asked. "We don't have any

suspects yet."

"Well, Justus said the man has dark hair and bought drinks for that Cody guy," Scotty spoke up. "Based on that and what happened to me, my money is on Andy."

"We can't rule out Dean, either," Justus added.

"But we need more to go on than that," Marcus said and shoulder bumped Scotty beside him. "We need more proof, maybe someone who could positively identify the guy."

"Patrick," Justus spoke up.

"Patrick? Who's Patrick?" Dale asked.

"He saw the guy Cody left with," Justus answered and looked around the club. Across the dance floor he spotted Curtis talking to a cowboy. "Be right back."

Before anyone could stop him, Justus jumped up and headed across the club. Weaving around the clusters of men standing about, Justus reached the other side of the dance floor but lost sight of Curtis.

"Damn!" He looked around and then approached the bartender. "Hey, did you see where Curtis went?"

The bartender continued to fill a tall mug with tap beer. He scanned the crowd then shook his head.

"Thanks." Justus returned to the table where his friends were seated.

"What was that about?" Scotty asked.

"Last Monday, when I heard about that Cody guy, his two friends Curtis and Patrick were coming here. I saw Curtis a second ago and tried to catch him. Maybe he knows something."

"Did he?" Dale asked.

"I lost him," Justus admitted.

"Well, before we go around asking people for information, maybe we should get a picture of Andy and Dean to show them?" Scotty suggested.

"How can we do that?" Justus asked. "They don't allow people to take photos in the clubs. It's a sort of a what-happens-in-here-stays-in-here rule."

"Well, they can't stop all of us. We can all try and whoever gets a pic can text it to the rest," Scotty explained.

"I'm good with that," Marcus spoke up, a bit distracted by someone across the room. "See you later," he said and left with his drink in hand.

"Well, there he goes again," Dale groused.

"What do you care?" Scotty snapped.

"I thought we were supposed to hang together tonight," Dale answered.

"Come on guys, don't argue," Justus interrupted. "We all know what Marcus is like. We can still have fun."

"Whatever," Dale said and took a drink of his beer.

"I need another Coke," Scotty said and looked around for the server.

"When are you going to have something stronger?" Dale asked.

"I don't need anything stronger," Scotty answered. "Alcohol makes my head hurt."

"Then you aren't drinking enough of it," Dale teased, though it sounded more like a jab to Justus. "Honestly, how do you ever expect to find yourself a man and get laid if you don't loosen up a bit?"

"I don't need a man," Scotty said while he stared at someone or something across the bar. Justus turned to see but only saw Marcus talking to some rugged cowboy-type guy. He looked back at Scotty who appeared sullen.

"What are you doing in a gay bar then?" Dale continued.

"What's that supposed to mean?" Scotty asked.

"The only reason to come here is to pick up a guy."

"Maybe for you, but I like watching people and the music and—"

"A voyeur!" Dale shrieked and laughed. "You little perve, you! All this innocent act—"

"I didn't mean like that," Scotty snapped. He turned and grabbed his jacket from the back of his chair. "I've had enough. I'm going home."

"No, wait!" Justus said. He grabbed Scotty's arm and stopped him.

"I'm sorry, I was only teasing," Dale said.

"Well, it didn't sound like it."

"Scott, you know I didn't mean it."

"Maybe I don't," Scotty answered.

"I'm sorry," Dale apologized and then quickly took a gulp of his beer. Justus figured it was to wash the bitter taste of apology out of his mouth. He laughed inside.

Scotty stood with his jacket in one hand and Justus' hand still gripping his other forearm. "Fine," he said and returned to his seat.

Justus spotted a server heading toward them. He signaled for him.

"Howdy, gents, what can I get you?" the blonde-haired man asked. Even though he was dressed like a cowboy, Justus thought he looked too pretty to be a real one.

"I'll have a rum and Coke," Justus ordered.

"Another beer for me," Dale said.

"And a Coke for our friend," Justus added and looked pleadingly at Scotty.

Scotty slipped his coat over the back of his chair.

"Coming right up," the server said before heading back to the bar.

"Thanks, Scotty," Justus said.

"No problem." Scotty sounded depressed.

"Wasn't the Saint Paddy's Day Bash crazy?" Dale spoke up.

Justus' mouth dropped open and he elbowed Dale in the ribs.

"Ouch! What was that for?" Dale grimaced and rubbed his side.

"We're not talking about that," Justus snapped.

"Oh! I totally forgot. I'm sorry, Scotty."

"Forget it. I'm over it," Scotty said indifferently and shrugged his shoulders.

"I wouldn't be," Dale continued. "I mean, talk about your psycho, Justus, Scotty's guy should be at the top of the list!"

"Really, Dale?" Justus said, sounding exasperated.

"Yes. The way he lured poor Scotty to his house in the West Hills, the way his mood changed when Scotty put on the brakes, that screams crazy man."

The image of Andy outside Stumptown flashed in Justus' mind. Andy did have dark hair and was not too bad looking, but there was nothing memorable about him. Maybe Dale had something?

"Here you go," the server greeted, interrupting Justus' thoughts and Dale's rambling. The server began setting the drinks on the table.

The three pulled out their money to pay for them. The server took Justus' and Dale's money, but when Scotty tried to pay for his, the server held up his hand.

"No, it's on the house."

"But—"

"We here at CC's let designated drivers drink for free, as long as it's nonalcoholic."

"Well, thank you," Scotty said, sounding surprised and

pleased at the same time.

"Don't mention it," the server smiled and gave him a wink before heading off to another table.

"Looks like you hit the jackpot here," Justus said.

Scotty shrugged his shoulders and took a sip of his Coke. His cheeks turned a little darker shade of pink.

"So, what do you think?" Dale asked.

"About what?" Scotty asked.

"About Andy?"

"Can we drop it for now," Justus interrupted.

"Fine," Dale said but sounded anything but. "What do you suppose he does with them?"

"Damn it, Dale," Justus groaned.

"Hey, we need to talk about this if we're going to find them."

Justus looked at Scotty who gave him a nod. "Okay. I don't know."

"Well, didn't you say the guys who abducted Harrison's friend were part of a ring that sold their captives into slavery on fishing boats?"

"Yes, but we're not on the coast," Justus said.

"We don't have to be. He could haul them off to Astoria or someplace in the back of a semi or moving van."

Scotty's eyes widened.

"No, I don't think it's the same thing," Justus answered. "As much as I hate to think about it, I think it may be worse."

"Worse? What could be worse than being knee deep in fish guts in the bottom of a stinking ship?" Dale asked.

"Dead," Scotty said, the color draining from his cheeks.

Justus nodded. He was glad he did not have to say the word. It had been in his mind ever since day one. He had no reason to think it. It had merely been a gut feeling he had kept to himself, until now.

Dale glared at Scotty. His jaw tightened and his lips pressed thin in an angry frown. Only his eyes, damp with tears, showed his true feelings.

"You don't know what you're talking about," he snapped. "Neither of you!"

He jumped to his feet, grabbed his drink and pushed through the small crowd.

"Dale!" Scotty called to him, but Dale did not respond.

Justus watched him walk over to the bar and gulp down the rest of his drink before giving the bartender his empty glass. They said something to each other and Dale turned around and left the club.

"I didn't mean to upset him," Scotty said.

"It's okay. I think we're all thinking the same thing. Only we didn't want to admit it out loud."

"Do you really think Andy has something to do with this?"

"I don't know. You did say his house smelled, so maybe. But, it could be Dean."

"Why are all the pyschos so hot?"

"I don't know. Most killers are. I remember when I was in middle school; there were two girls in my class who were murdered by a neighbor. It was all over the news. He was even interviewed when the first girl disappeared. I don't remember his connection to them but he killed them and then buried them under his patio."

"Under his patio?"

"Yeah," Justus agreed. He drank the rest of his rum and Coke. "He told the police he was enlarging his cement patio when they did a search of his property. They had no idea he was really covering up where they were buried."

"How'd the police figure it out?" Scotty asked.

"I don't remember. I think he was turned in by a family member or someone. The police never suspected him as far as I knew."

"Do you think Dale remembers that?"

Justus looked across the club at the door. "I have no idea."

The clock in the dining room struck eleven when Justus walked through the front door. The light in the living room was on and the TV was airing Harrison's favorite movie.

"You're home early," Harrison commented from the sofa. "Is everything okay?"

Justus walked over to the archway and leaned against the threshold. His arms were folded over his chest. Harrison sat up and turned the volume on the TV down.

"Yeah," he answered.

"That didn't sound like it. What happened? Did you run into Dean again?"

"No. Thank heaven. Remember I told you about a third guy who's missing?"

Harrison nodded. He turned the TV off and set the remote on the coffee table.

"Since the police don't seem to be doing anything about it, the guys and I were talking about what we should do."

Harrison started shaking his head. "No. No," he said. "Justus, stay out of it."

"I think it's a little late for that."

"Why? What have you done?"

"Nothing. . . yet. One of Cody's friends saw the man he left the club with."

"Has he given a description to the police?"

"No, and I don't think he will as long as he listens to Cherry Royale and Curtis. As I was saying, based on the description Patrick gave me and what we know about the first guy that disappeared, we've narrowed the suspect list down to two guys, Andy and Dean."

Harrison looked confused. "Why them?"

"Well, after what happened to Scotty, Andy is creepy enough and the way Dean is stalking me, need I say more?"

Harrison let out a loud sigh. "Justus, I don't like this. You should tell the police what you know and let them handle it."

"Isn't that being a little hypocritical? I mean, you didn't leave it to them to find Thomas."

"That was different."

"Dale doesn't think so. He thinks these disappearances might be tied in with the people who took Thomas."

Harrison shook his head again. "I seriously doubt it. Judd Hanks and his family are all locked up somewhere."

"Yeah, but couldn't it be another—"

"No," Harrison interrupted. "It would be too risky to run an operation like that this far from the ocean or a seaport. Besides, the Feds assured me that Portland wasn't on the list of cities where men were being shanghaied."

"Oh." Justus nodded in agreement. Inside, his fear that Jack was dead grew stronger. "That's what I thought, too."

"You did? So, what do you think happened to them?" Harrison asked with a puzzled look.

Justus took a deep breath and let it out slowly in the hope that it would calm him somehow. It did not. "I don't think we'll ever find them—alive, anyway."

Harrison nodded. It was not the reaction Justus had expected.

"What? You don't think so either?" he asked.

"I haven't said anything, but that thought has crossed my mind."

"It's also crossed the others, even though Dale won't admit it."

"Why? What did he say?"

"It's not so much what he said as what he did. When Scotty said what we all were thinking, Dale got upset and left. He had tears in his eyes."

"I see," Harrison said. "But this is all speculation at this point. Who knows, these disappearances could be totally unrelated. Jack could have had enough of Portland and decided to move on. Those other men, I don't know. I don't know them."

"Yeah," Justus agreed but inside he could not shake the bad feeling he had.

"Just give it more time," Harrison said. "Let the police do their thing."

Justus did not say a word. He turned around and headed for his room upstairs.

"Good night," Harrison called after him.

CHAPTER TEN

The week seemed to fly by for Justus. Friday arrived and it was time to put their plan into action. The gang had agreed to meet at Stumptown, a decision that pleased Dale and he had not been shy about letting everyone know it. However, Justus was not sure if Dale understood the purpose of their return or how much help he would be in executing their plan. At least he could count on Scotty and Marcus.

The heavy beat of the classic dance music that greeted Justus when he entered the club felt like a giant hug. It was a far better feeling than the one the country-western crap at CC's gave him. He quickly made his way over to the gang's usual table and sat down. He was the first to arrive.

"What can I get you?" The server was standing on the dance floor and with his hand on the rail.

"A Captain Morgan's and Coke," Justus answered.

The server nodded and headed across the club to the bar.

While he waited for his drink and the others to arrive,

Justus looked around the club at the other men who were standing about with their drinks in hand. Their faces were familiar even though he did not know most of their names. He had seen them here and thought of them as regulars. There was no sign of either Dean or Andy.

"Here you go," the server said, setting the plain glass tumbler on the table in front of Justus. "So where are your friends tonight?" he asked.

Justus quickly pulled his money out of the pocket of his tight, skinny jeans and unfolded it for the server. "They're coming."

"No pun intended?" the server grinned.

Justus laughed and gave the server the once over. "We'll see."

"Okay. Let me know when you're ready. . . for another drink." He winked and then moved on to the next table.

Justus watched him for a moment, letting his mind undress the guy. He had a nice, well-defined body, in Justus' head anyway.

"Hey there," Dale called while he crossed the dance floor with his beer glass in hand. He ducked under the rail, something the bartenders and staff frowned on, and slipped into his chair.

"Well, you seem in a good mood," Justus greeted him and gave him an air kiss on both cheeks.

"Where're the others? I thought Scotty and Marcus would have been here by now."

"Don't know. Have you tried texting them?"

"Nah," Dale grunted and took a drink of his beer.

"So, can I count on you to help with our plan?"

"Sure," Dale answered but his body language did most of the talking. Justus nodded to himself knowingly. Dale was not going to help at all.

"Hi guys," Scotty said when he arrived at the table. He sat down across from Justus, leaving the chair between him and the rail for Marcus. Marcus loved to keep his eye on the crowd and sitting near the rail to the dance floor gave him a better vantage point.

The server came back and took Scotty's order. He winked at Justus again which caused Justus' groin to stir even though it was confined in his tight jeans.

Marcus arrived after the second round of drinks. He offered no excuse for being late but settled into his usual place at the table. Justus noticed that he seemed distracted and not by some hot guy somewhere in the club.

"Everything okay?" he asked.

"Everything's great," Marcus answered. Justus did not believe him but decided not to pursue it. Instead, he watched Marcus look around the club. "Are you sure they're going to show?"

"I hope so," Justus answered. He glanced at the bar and felt less positive. There was still no sign of either of them.

The four drank and chatted. The more Dale drank the more he tried to tempt Scotty into having something stronger than Coke. To Justus' surprise, Marcus did not leave the table to seek out his next conquest. He seemed content to stay with the group, something he had never done before. It was beginning to worry Justus.

Dean walked into the club at half past ten. Marcus was the first to notice and silenced the others. They watched while Dean walked straight to the bar and collected a drink. Justus felt his body vibrate deep inside.

"Okay, who's going to do it?" Marcus asked.

No one moved or answered. The three looked at Justus.

"He's your friend—"

"No, he's not!" Justus snapped at Dale. "But since you're all chicken, I guess I'll do it."

Justus took out his phone and readied the camera app. He tried to discreetly hold it up from his seat but in the dim light, he was too far away to get a clear shot.

"Be right back," he said and stood up.

"Be careful," Scotty warned. "If you're caught, they'll confiscate your phone or throw you out."

"I will," Justus answered. He slowly made his way through the crowd, keeping one eye on Dean and the other on the bouncer by the front door. Dean turned and began talking with someone beside him which gave Justus a good shot of his face. Justus held up his phone and readied his finger over the camera icon while he waited for it to focus on Dean.

"Oh no, you don't!" someone said from beside him and grabbed the phone out of his hand.

Justus turned sharply and looked at the person. It was the cute server.

"Give me back my phone."

"You know the rules," the server said through tight lips. "No pictures."

"I know," Justus admitted. "But I need to get this shot. He could be the guy responsible for the disappearances."

"Disappearances?" the server repeated and looked past Justus in Dean's direction. "Are you sure?"

"No, but I know someone who is and I need to show him that guy's picture."

The server looked at Justus and smiled. "I'm sorry. Those are the rules and if I let you do it, then I could be fired."

"Fine. I won't take his picture," Justus answered. "You can give me back my phone."

The server slipped the phone down the front of his rather

tight jeans. "You can claim it later," he said and winked at Justus. "See me in the back hall in twenty minutes. I have a break then."

Justus' jaw dropped and his mouth gaped. He could not believe this guy.

"Fine," he answered and headed back to the table.

"So?" Scotty asked. "Did you get it?"

"No," Justus said and dropped down into his chair. "That server caught me and took my phone."

"You were warned," Dale said in an I-told-you-so sort of way, but Scotty, not Dale, had been the one to warn him.

Justus ignored him and looked at the empty place next to Scotty. "Where's Marcus?"

"Don't know. He left right after you did," Scotty answered.

"Got it," Marcus said while he walked up to the table and took his place again.

"What? How?" Justus asked.

"While you and the server were playing hide the phone, I was able to get a clean shot of your guy."

"Great!" Justus said. "Text it to us—No, not yet. The server has my phone in his pants and I have it set on vibrate."

Dale laughed and pulled out his phone. His thumbs rapidly tapped at the screen.

"What are you doing?" Justus asked.

"You'll see," he answered. "Where's the server?" Dale looked around. "There he is."

Before Justus could grab Dale's phone, Dale hit the send icon. Justus looked at the server who stood by a table balancing a tray of drinks in one hand. Suddenly the server jumped and the tray tipped. The glasses fell over, splashing the nearest guy who jumped to his feet, knocking over his chair. There were words exchanged, but Justus could not hear what was said. The server quickly grabbed the bar towel that hung from his belt and handed it to the man. He glanced over his shoulder toward Justus and glared before stooping to clean up the mess.

Dale roared with laughter. Justus punched him hard in the shoulder.

"You trying to get me kicked out of here, asshole?" he snapped.

"Hey, he's the one who put your phone down his pants."

"I don't care. That's not funny," Justus said while Dale continued to laugh.

When the server finished cleaning up the floor and replacing the drinks, he walked over to their table.

"That will be twenty-five dollars," he said and held out his hand.

"For what?" Dale asked in a snide tone.

"For the drinks you caused me to drop."

"Hey that's on you," Dale answered and laughed at his own pun.

"It's either that or you all get thrown out of here and banned from ever coming back."

"You can't do that," Dale objected.

"Wanna bet?" the server answered.

"Pay him," Marcus said, looking straight at Dale.

"Me? Why me?"

"You sent the text," Justus answered.

Dale looked around the table. "Fine," he answered and pulled out his wallet. He handed the server the money.

The server reached down the front of his jeans and pulled out Justus' phone. He set it on the table. "Forget about meeting me," he said. "Next time, I'll call the bouncer." He walked away.

"That was really stupid," Scotty said, turning to look at Dale.

"Why? It didn't cost you anything and Justus got his phone back."

"Yeah, but you nearly got us all kicked out of here."

"Eh, forget it. He wasn't going to do anything."

"Stop it, both of you," Marcus spoke up. "We still have to get a picture of Scotty's Andy. Look around. Do you see him?"

It was nearly closing time and Andy had not showed up. Justus felt good that they had gotten Dean's pic. He could find Patrick and show him that at least.

"I'm going to call it a night," Scotty said and started to put on his jacket.

"Yeah, me too," Marcus said. "Need a cab, Dale?"

Dale looked up with half-closed, glassy eyes. "Huh?" he grunted.

"I take that as a yes," Marcus answered.

"I'll take him home," Justus offered.

"Okay," Marcus said while he stood up.

The four made their way outside to the quiet of the street. They said their goodbyes and headed off in different directions. Justus helped Dale into the passenger seat of his car.

"I can drive," Dale slurred and leaned toward the steering wheel.

"Spoken like a true drunk," Justus said with a hint of anger in his tone. He shut the passenger door and hurried around to the driver's side.

"Hi, Justus," a deep voice said from the shadows.

Justus recognized it immediately and shuddered. He looked up right when Dean stepped out of the shadows.

"Picking up drunks now?" Dean asked, sounding a bit

hostile.

"No. I'm taking my friend Dale home. You remember him."

Dean bent down and looked thought the window. "Ah, yes," he said and laughed. "Had a little too much tonight."

"And every week since one of our friends went missing, but I suppose you have no idea about that," Justus said in an accusing sort of tone. He felt a little bolder with the car between them.

Dean furrowed his brow and shook his head. "No, I don't. I heard talk about some guys. When? What happened?" he asked.

Justus heard the concern in Dean's voice. It sounded sincere and for a moment threw him off. He did not know what to say. Dale suddenly honked the horn and caused both Justus and Dean to jump.

"I'll let you go," Dean said. "Good night, drive carefully."

Justus did not respond. He threw the driver's door open. "Get back over there," he said while he pushed Dale back over onto the passenger's side. He slipped into the driver's seat and shut the door. Looking out the passenger window, he did not see any sign of Dean. He was gone.

It was well past four in the morning when Justus pulled up to the curb in front of Harrison's house in Northeast Portland. He shut off the engine and sat for a moment listening to the quiet and looking around the neighborhood. Everything seemed peaceful, with the still cars parked in the many driveways and against the curb, and the dark windows of the houses. In the distance, Justus spotted someone on a bicycle coming toward him. He watched the paperboy tossing his load of newspapers one at a time while he rode up the street. Justus stepped out of his car and waited on the curb.

"Morning," he called as the boy drew near and readied to throw Harrison's paper toward the house.

The boy was startled. He swerved and for a moment lost his balance, but righted himself at the last moment before falling over.

"Sorry," Justus apologized and felt bad for the boy.

The boy threw the paper but did not respond. It landed on the walk behind Justus. Then he pedaled away a little faster.

Justus turned around and picked up the paper. While he made is way up the walk, he fumbled with his keys. It was not until he started up the front steps that he noticed a light on inside. *That's odd. Harrison never leaves a light on for me.* Opening the front door, Justus heard a raised voice coming from the kitchen. Harrison sounded angry at someone. Justus slowly closed and locked the front door behind him.

"I don't care what you believe. I told you, I haven't heard from her," Harrison shouted.

Justus cringed. He tiptoed toward the stairs. The floor creaked loudly and he stopped. He glanced in the direction of the kitchen. Harrison stood leaning against the archway between the kitchen and dining room with the telephone to his ear. He nodded when their eyes met and then stood up sharply.

"Why would I do that?" he snapped at the caller. "Don't give me that, you know damned well you're not innocent. How many times—I don't care if you *are* their father. That doesn't give you the right to lay a hand on them. —You're right, I wasn't there and you should be thankful I wasn't because chief of police or not—Oh grow up, little man." Harrison sneered then disconnected the call. He walked back into the dining room and slammed his cell phone face down on the table.

Justus put off going upstairs and slowly walked over to the dining room. He stood behind his chair at the end of the table and put his hands on its back.

"I'd hate to be the person on the other end," he said and tried to smile. "I take it that was your brother-in-law?"

Harrison nodded and took a deep breath. "That's right," he said. "He still can't get it through his pea brain that I don't know where Danika is. He thinks I'm lying."

"Why did he call so early?" Justus responded, not knowing what else to say.

"He was out drinking with his buddies, and then called me, drunk," Harrison said and shook his head. "He thought if he caught me off guard I might slip and tell him where she is. That's not going to happen!" he shouted at the dead phone on the table.

"Because you don't know where she is, right?" Justus asked.

Harrison looked at him. "No, I don't know where she is," he answered in a calm but worried tone. "Even if I did, I wouldn't tell him."

"I guess it's a good thing he's calling you—"

"What?" Harrison snapped and gave Justus a sharp look.

"It means he has no clue where she is either. So she's safe."

"Oh," Harrison said. The creases between his eyebrows relaxed and his eyes sparkled a bit in the dim light of the chandelier. "You're right." He grinned. "I knew there was a reason I kept you around."

"Thanks, I think," Justus replied.

"So, did you have a good night? Did you get what you wanted?" Harrison changed the subject.

"Half of it. Marcus got a picture of Dean."

"Not the other guy?"

"He wasn't there."

"I see," Harrison said with a nod. "Coffee?"

"Sure, why not?" Justus answered. He knew he should be tired. He had not slept all night, but he felt wide awake.

Col. Mustard walked into the dining room from the hallway. He looked up at Justus and yowled as though telling Justus he woke him up.

"I'm sorry, Col. Mustard," Justus apologized.

Col. Mustard continued to stand by the hall and yowl.

"What? Are you hungry?" Justus continued talking to the cat. "Well, let's see if Harry's got anything for you."

He walked into the kitchen and Col. Mustard followed.

"I think he's hungry," Justus said.

"He's always hungry," Harrison answered and turned the coffee maker on to start brewing. "Coming right up," he told Col. Mustard and grabbed a can of cat food from the pantry.

"So, where's your hunky boyfriend?" Justus asked while he grabbed the orange juice pitcher from the top shelf in the fridge. "Leave early?"

"He left last night after we watched a movie and you know he's not my *boyfriend*," Harrison corrected him, sounding exasperated. He peeled the lid off the can and Col. Mustard started to meow louder and pace the floor by his water dish.

"Well, he's a boy and he's a friend," Justus commented.

"He's hardly a boy," Harrison corrected.

"Ha!" Justus gave a triumphant laugh.

"Not everyone is gay, Justus."

"In my world they are."

"You know Douglas has a lady friend. He's not into guys."

"If you say so."

"I do," Harrison answered and spooned the cat food into a crystal-cut, glass bowl.

"What about you?" Justus asked.

Harrison stopped and gave Justus one of his looks. "I'm not going to answer that again."

"That's okay." Justus smiled and took a sip of his orange juice.

Outside the sun had begun to rise. Justus walked around the island and sat down on one of the stools.

"Hungry? I can fix us some scrambled eggs?" Harrison asked after he gave Col. Mustard his food.

"Got any ham left?"

"I think so."

Justus noticed Harrison's hand shaking when he picked an egg out of the carton.

"Are you okay?" he asked.

"I'm fine. I guess I'm still upset over the phone call. You want toast?" Harrison asked.

"Sure," Justus replied. He watched Harrison drop two slices of bread into the toaster. Justus knew his roommate well enough to know that not knowing where Danika was or if she was safe was torture. Besides him, Danika and her boys were Harrison's only family. At least that is how Justus felt about Harrison, family.

The scrambled eggs ended up turning into ham and cheese omelets by the time Harrison finished cooking. He handed a plate to Justus and they carried their food into the dining room and sat down at the table. Justus looked at his omelet and took in a deep breath of the aroma. Harrison was a wonderful cook, something Justus wished he were. His attempt at making French toast had resulted in soggy, burnt bread and a kitchen that looked as though a flour bomb had gone off. After that, Harrison had forbidden him from ever cooking again.

"Slow down, it's not a race," Harrison said.

Justus looked up and sat back in his chair. He set his fork down and picked up his coffee cup. It was true; he did tend to eat quickly. It was a habit he had picked up a long time ago while growing up at home with his parents and three older sisters. Among the four of them, they had an understanding—the last one to finish eating had to wash the dishes. It took Justus quite a while to figure out how, but he was able to finish first and finally beat his sisters. It was now a habit that proved hard to break.

"So, how are Scotty and the guys?" Harrison tried to make conversation while he took small, leisurely bites.

"Scotty seems to be fine, back to his normal self. Dale is still drinking way too much, but it's Marcus I'm worried about."

"Really?" Harrison asked, sounding surprised. "Why?"

"He's been acting a bit off lately."

"How so?"

"He asked me a week or so ago to be the executor of his will."

Harrison shrugged indifferently. "That's normal. I mean, when someone owns property and has money it's the responsible thing to do."

Justus looked at Harrison as a thought hit him. "So, do you have a will?"

"I do," Harrison answered and took a sip from his coffee cup.

"Really?"

"Yes."

"So, who's your executor?"

"Douglas."

"Oh, of course," Justus said and grinned.

Harrison squinted and cocked his head. "So, is that the only reason you're concerned about Marcus?"

"No," Justus answered and his expression sobered. "Tonight, he seemed different. He was quieter and he stayed with us all night. He didn't go off to find a hookup like he normally does."

"Well, I wouldn't worry about it too much. It's probably nothing. He'll be back to his old self in no time."

"I suppose."

The two finished their breakfast and then Justus went upstairs to bed.

CHAPTER ELEVEN

When Justus phoned the group about wanting to stop by CC's to see if he could show the pic of Dean to Patrick, he was surprised when all of them, even Dale, suggested meeting there instead of Stumptown. Ever since Justus had taken him home the Friday before, Dale seemed more amiable. Probably due to his guilt over being stupid-drunk that night, Justus figured. Whatever the reason, he was glad when he walked into the club and spotted the gang all waiting at a table in the corner away from the dance floor.

"What took you so long?" Scotty asked when Justus sat down beside Dale.

"I had trouble finding parking. The church people have the parking strip in front of their church blocked off for some reason."

"I noticed that," Scotty said. "Wonder if it has to do with Lent."

"Isn't that a Catholic thing?" Dale asked.

"Presbyterians do it too, sort of," Marcus answered.

"Whatever it is, it's annoying trying to find a parking spot."

"So, what can I get you?" a server in a suede leather vest and cowboy hat asked. His voice was deep and manly. It made Justus feel tingly all over.

"I'll have a. . ." Justus thought quickly of another drink that sounded more butch than a rum and Coke. "Jack Daniel's. Make it a double."

The server smiled and walked away. Justus let his eyes linger a bit before turning back to the shocked faces of his friends.

"Since when do you drink whiskey?" Marcus asked.

"And a double shot at that!" Dale chimed in.

"Since the server looks like that," Justus said and looked across the club. The server stood leaning across the bar which made his jeans tighter and showed off his firm ass.

"Down, boy," Scotty said.

"Sure!" Justus laughed and turned back to his friends.

"Oh, before I forget, I bought us all tickets to Stumptown's Easter Bash on the nineteenth," Dale spoke up.

"How much?"

"Nothing," Dale said and stopped Marcus from pulling out his wallet. "My treat."

"You don't have to do that," Justus told him.

"I know. I want to."

"What's gotten into you?" Scotty asked.

"Nothing. I simply thought it was time to move on. That's all."

"Uh-oh, what happened?" Justus said. He could tell something was up with Dale.

"Nothing," Dale answered with a nervous sounding

laugh.

The other three stared at him as though saying they did not believe him.

"Fine," Dale relented. "Jack's parents came and cleared out Jack's apartment last weekend."

"What?" they all let out a collective gasp.

"It was bound to happen. It's been three months." Dale's voice cracked and belied his brave front.

"Oh, Dale, I'm so sorry," Justus said and put his arm around Dale's shoulders.

Dale shrugged it off. "Hey, he was only a friend. We weren't lovers or—" He looked down at his lap.

Justus looked across the table at Scotty and Marcus.

"It doesn't mean anything," Marcus said firmly. "So, they cleaned out his apartment. Big deal. They may have given up on finding him, but we haven't."

"That's right," Scotty agreed. "We are going to find him."

Dale looked up, this time with tears in his eyes. "Thanks guys, but we all know he's probably gone for good."

"Who's gone?" the server's deep voice resonated.

Justus looked beside him at the handsome specimen of cowboy-hood. He felt his legs go weak and was grateful to be sitting.

"A friend," he answered.

"There seems to be a lot of that lately," the server commented and nodded. "I know of a couple others. One guy from here. I sure wish the police would do something."

"Don't we all," Scotty agreed.

"Who was your friend?"

"Jack," Dale spoke up, his composure restored. "He disappeared from Stumptown's Valentine's Day party."

"Oh my. And no one has done anything?"

"I went to the police," Justus volunteered. "But they dropped it. We're not, though."

"Well, good. Someone needs to do something."

"How much do I owe you?" Justus asked and looked at the drink on the server's tray.

The man shuddered slightly as if coming back to the present and his job. "Oh, nothing," he answered and set the drink on the table in front of Justus. "We can work something out later. Name's Xavier."

"Xavier," Justus repeated.

"Yeah, my parents and their sense of humor," Xavier said and shook his head. "Xavier Yancy Zervis, X Y Z."

"I rather like it," Justus said.

Xavier smiled. "If you need anything more, let me know."

"I'll do that."

After Xavier left, Justus looked back at the group.

"Good God, can you be any more obvious? You need a napkin to wipe your chin?" Marcus laughed.

"What?" Justice asked, feigning innocence.

"What? You all but did him right here at the table."

Justus felt his face turn red, not from embarrassment as much as from Marcus seeming to read his mind.

"Forget about him," Justus said. "Tonight, we need to be watching for Patrick."

"And how are we supposed to do that?" Scotty asked. "We've never met him and don't know what he looks like."

"Oh, yeah, well. . ." Justus stammered. Scotty was right. He was the only one who had seen Patrick. "I'll keep an eye out."

As the night wore on, Marcus took his drink and began making the rounds, on the prowl for some fresh meat for the night. Even Dale was on the hunt but from time to time checked back with Justus and Scotty to see if Patrick had arrived.

"How did we ever become friends?" Scotty lamented.

"What? You and me?" Justus asked.

"No, them," he laughed.

Justus looked over his shoulder toward the last place he saw Dale. "Oh!" he gasped.

"What? He's here?" Scotty asked and began to look the crowd over.

"No, but someone equally as good," Justus answered. "Stay here. I'll be right back."

Keeping an eye on Curtis, Justus made his way across the club. Curtis stood at the end of the bar talking with one of the bartenders. Justus tried not to eavesdrop while he waited for them to finish. Finally, Curtis glanced over his shoulder and noticed him.

"Hey, aren't you that guy from a couple weeks ago? The one with the missing friend?" he said, turning around and smiling.

"Yes," Justus said with a nod. "I was wondering if you know where I could find Patrick."

"He's at home. He's too frightened to come clubbing anymore. He's afraid that guy will come back for him."

"Well, that's what I wanted to talk to him about. You see, my friends and I have started our own investigation since it doesn't appear the police are doing anything."

"Really?" Curtis said with a smirk and leaned a little closer. "What have you got?"

Justus could tell he was being mocked, and that Curtis thought it was a joke. Still, he had to know if Dean was the guy.

"I have a picture I wanted to show Patrick."

"I bet," Curtis said in a condescending tone.

"No," Justus almost shouted the word. "It's of a guy who's been stalking me and I wanted to see if it was the guy Patrick saw the night his friend disappeared."

"Well, show me," Curtis said.

Justus hesitated a moment. "Maybe I could text it to him?"

"That's not going to happen, but you can text it to me. I'll show him and then let you know what he says."

Justus hesitated while he thought. He was not sure if he really trusted Curtis to do what he said. After all, he did not know him and from the way he acted the other night. . .

"Fine," Justus said. He opened his photo app and attached Dean's photo to a text. "What's your number?"

"Here," Curtis said and took Justus' cell phone. He keyed in his cell number and sent the text. Justus heard Curtis' phone chime. Curtis then deleted the text from Justus' phone so Justus would not have a record of his number. He handed the cell back to Justus and took out his phone. He looked at the photo text. "Nice looking daddy, if you're into that." He gave Justus a once over look. "You can go now."

Justus did not move. He was in shock over how rude Curtis was. He wanted to tell him what he could do to himself but figured he probably already did and did not need any encouragement. He turned around and headed back to his table.

"So, how did it go?" Scotty asked.

"He's going to show Patrick the pic and let me know."

"That's good isn't it?"

"Yeah," Justus answered.

"Then why aren't you happy?"

"Curtis is a dried up, bitchy queen is why. The way he talked down to me and how he acted. I could tell he thinks I'm only a stupid little twink."

"Forget about him," Scotty said and stood up. "Your server friend stopped by and said his shift ended. He wants you to wait for him outside. I've got to get going myself."

"What about the others?" Justus asked and looked around the dwindling crowd.

"Marcus took off with some guy."

"Dark hair?"

"No, blonde." Scotty sighed while they headed for the door. "And Dale headed home with that cowboy he was riding in the corner. Call me tomorrow?"

"Sure," Justus said. He watched Scotty walk away, heading south on 12th Avenue toward his condo. A bell in one of the many church towers struck. Justus jumped and then looked at his watch.

The early morning air was a bit cold. Justus had left his jacket in his car and now wished he had brought it. He began to pace up and down the sidewalk a few steps while he waited for Xavier.

He did not have to wait too long. The door to CC's opened and Xavier walked out wearing a leather jacket and baseball cap. He smiled when he saw Justus and immediately headed over to him.

"So, where's your cowboy outfit?" Justus asked.

Xavier laughed. "My uniform stays here. These are my real clothes." He opened the front of his jacket to reveal a black T-shirt. His jeans were tight in all the right places.

"Well, now what?" Justus asked.

"You wanna go to my place?"

"Sure. Where is it?"

"It's not far. I have a house in Cedar Mills."

"Okay, should I follow you?"

"No, we can take my car and then I can bring you back

downtown."

"Sounds like a plan."

The sun was already beginning to rise by the time Justus made it home. He opened the front door and was struck by the aroma of sizzling bacon and fresh hot coffee. His stomach grumbled and came to life. He closed the door and headed for the kitchen.

"Good morning," he greeted and froze. "Oh!"

Douglas turned around, spatula in hand. He smiled at Justus. "Morning," he said.

"Where're your clothes?"

"What? You don't like my boxers and Harry's apron?"

"No, no," Justus answered. "I—I—"

"Coffee?" Douglas offered and held up the pot.

"Sure," Justus answered and forced himself to look away from his crush. He grabbed his mug from the cupboard and let Douglas fill it.

"Cream?" Douglas asked.

Justus looked at the bulge in the front of Douglas' apron and instantly his face felt hot. He knew it was turning red.

Douglas laughed and handed him the bottle of sweet cream. He turned back to the stove and put another four strips of bacon in the pan.

"So, where's Harry?" Justus asked, finding his voice.

"He's still asleep I think."

"Oh. Did you spend the night?"

"In Thomas' room," Douglas answered and turned back around. He picked up his coffee cup and took a sip.

"Thomas' room," Justus repeated. "When are we going to stop calling it that?"

Douglas did not answer. "Hey, Harry told me about what

you're doing," he changed the subject.

"Yeah?" Justus did not know why he was so surprised. He knew Harrison told Douglas practically everything.

"I wish you guys wouldn't. I know it's hard letting the police handle it, but you should. It's too dangerous."

"Like you did last year?"

"I know," Douglas nodded. "That's why I'm telling you now. You're a good friend and I don't want anything to happen to you."

Friend. Justus' mind caught on the word. It was not the first time Douglas had called him his friend, but it was the first time he had done it dressed in boxers and little else. It seemed to make the word sound more special.

"Well, we're being careful," Justus said, trying to reassure him.

"I thought I heard talking," Harrison said when he walked into the kitchen.

Justus turned to look at him and halfway expected to see Harrison in his shorts. Instead, he was dressed in jeans and one of his *comfortable* but worn sweatshirts.

"Morning," Justus greeted.

"Just getting in?" Harrison asked while he poured himself a cup of coffee.

"Yeah."

"So, how did it go last night?"

"Great. I met this hot guy and he took me to his place in Cedar Mills. He showed me his huge—"

"Spare me the details!" Harrison interrupted. His face was already turning red.

"His huge house," Justus laughed. "What did you think I was going to say?"

"Never mind," Harrison answered.

"Well, that was huge too."

Harrison choked on his coffee and turned toward the sink. Douglas patted him on the back.

"Damn it, Justus!" Harrison cursed when he regained his voice.

"Sorry." Justus said and tried not to laugh. "It wasn't all that great, just so you know. The guy was hot enough but not someone I'd want as a friend."

"Really? Why?" Douglas asked.

"While we drove to his place, he told me he owned the house. Turned out it was his parents' house and they were out of town for the weekend."

"How did you find that out?"

"They came home early. We heard them. Xavier—that's his name—panicked and had me climb out his bedroom window. He threw down my clothes and I had to get dressed in the shadows." Justus avoided looking at Douglas. He could tell Douglas was trying not to laugh and doing a poor job of it. "Then I had to walk two miles to the nearest TriMet stop and catch a bus back downtown to my car."

"I'm sorry," Harrison said while he too tried to stifle a laugh.

"It's okay, it's not like we weren't finished." Justus shifted his weight on the stool.

"Well, maybe next time—"

"No," Justus interrupted Douglas. "There's no *next times*. They get one shot—"

"So, moving right along," Harrison interrupted. "Did you find the guy and show him the picture?"

"No," Justus answered. "But I did find a friend of his who said he'd show him the pic. I'm not holding out any hope, though. The guy was a jerk."

"Well, maybe he'll do it." Harrison said.

"I hope so." Justus took a sip of his coffee. "He said he would text me."

CHAPTER TWELVE

Try as he might, Justus could not stop thinking about the picture and Patrick. It had been five days and still no text from Curtis. He was beginning to think he was right, that Curtis was not going to show Patrick the picture.

Justus glanced at the flowers in the garbage can beside his desk in the file room. Dean still had not let up. Justus picked up the card and looked at the inscription again. The growing anxiety inside his chest was beginning to make him feel as if he were about to explode. He grabbed his coffee cup and headed for the break room.

The break room was located on the west side of the twenty-eighth floor overlooking the West Hills. It was not a large room, but it was not a closet either. A counter—complete with sink, microwave, and industrial coffee maker—spanned the wall to the right between the door and the windows. Several round tables surrounded by too many plastic chairs took up the center of the room. Against the wall to the left sat an uncomfortable, worn, and stained office couch with matching and equally stained chairs. No one ever sat on them anymore and Justus did not know why they were still taking up space.

Music from an easy listening station was piped in through the speakers in the ceiling and controlled by the main switch in the boss' office upstairs. Justus was told it eliminated fighting. He did not care for the station, in fact, with everything else that was on his mind, it grated on his nerves.

Justus walked straight over to the coffee urn and filled his cup. He looked in the small refrigerator for the bottle of sweet cream and took it out. It felt light. He shook it. Empty!

"Why don't they throw it out?" he grumbled and threw the plastic bottle into the trash. He grabbed his cup and headed back to his file room.

The telephone on his desk was ringing when he walked into the room. Justus nearly spilled his coffee while he hurried to answer it.

"Are you going to make your rounds anytime soon?" Harrison asked.

"Oh, yeah," Justus said. "Be right there."

He hung up the phone right when his cell phone rang. He grabbed it and answered without checking the caller ID.

"Hello?"

"Justus, this is Scotty. Have you heard from Marcus?"

"No. Not since last Friday."

"Neither have I. I tried calling his cell, but he's not answering. It goes straight to voicemail."

"Have you tried his work number?"

"Yes, but they said he hasn't been in."

"Hasn't been in?" Justus repeated and sat down in his chair. His stomach tightened and he suddenly felt nauseous. A sense of dread filled him. "I'll see what I can find out. Try not to worry. You know Marcus. He may have decided to take a few days off."

"Okay. Let me know when you find out anything."

"I will." Justus disconnected the call and quickly dialed Marcus' home phone. It rang and rang. He tried his cell number. As Scotty had said, the call went straight to voicemail. Justus stuck his phone in his pocket, grabbed his cart, and headed for Harrison's office.

"I was beginning to think—" Harrison stopped when he looked at Justus. "What is it? Did you hear from that guy?"

"No," Justus answered and shook his head. "Scotty called. He hasn't been able to reach Marcus."

"Is that normal?"

"Sort of, but he said he called Marcus' work and they told him Marcus hasn't been in all week."

"Oh."

"I'm worried."

"Well, when was the last time you saw him?"

"Friday night at CC's. He left with a guy."

"You don't think—"

"No. Scotty said the guy was blonde. The other man was dark haired." Justus sat down on the corner of Harrison's desk.

"Well, what do you want to do?" Harrison asked.

"I don't know. Can we go by his house on our way home?"

"Of course."

Justus looked at the clock. It was a quarter after three. "Can we leave now?"

Harrison looked as though he were about to object but then turned to his phone. He dialed a number Justus knew was the staffing office upstairs.

"I need to take Justus home early," Harrison said into the

receiver. "He's not feeling well. No, he can't take the bus. Okay, code it however you need. See you tomorrow." Harrison hung up the phone. "Done."

"Thanks."

On the drive to Marcus', Justus sent Scotty a quick text to let him know what he and Harrison were doing. Scotty acknowledged with a Thumbs Up emoji.

Marcus owned a two-story 1908 house in the Belmont District of Southeast Portland. The past November, he completed a two-year remodel project that included having a new foundation installed to bring the house up to code. He had hosted his first party two days after Christmas. With the house decorated to the nines, his guests showed their approval by showering him with the appropriate ooo's and ahh's.

Harrison pulled up to the curb in front of the house behind a Toyota Camry. He parked and turned off the engine.

"Looks like he's home," Justus said from the passenger seat of Harrison's Honda CR-V. "That's his car."

"But there aren't any lights on inside," Harrison said.

Justus turned and looked at the front of the house. The large picture window to the left of the front door and the two second-floor windows were indeed dark.

"Maybe he's in the kitchen or upstairs in his den, it's on the back," Justus speculated. "Let's go see."

He did not wait for Harrison to reply. He opened the car door and stepped out onto the sidewalk. He walked over to the gate in the picket fence and opened it. A large spring attached to the gate let it close by itself. Justus headed for the front door.

The small front lawn appeared neatly trimmed and the flowerbeds at the base of the front porch and around the lawn were picture perfect. Marcus had hired a gardener to take care of it all. Justus wished Harrison would do the same. He hated pulling weeds and raking the mountain of leaves that fell off the old oak trees in the front of Harrison's house.

When he reached the front door, Justus pressed the doorbell. The melodious sound of chimes rang out from inside. He listened quietly but heard no movement.

"Try it again," Harrison urged from behind Justus.

Justus did a quick three rings and listened. He noticed Harrison standing in front of the living room window to the left. His hands were cupped on either side of his face while he peered inside.

"It doesn't look like he's home," Harrison said, turning back to Justus. "Are you sure that's his car?"

"Positive," Justus said and pulled a key from his pocket.

"You have a key?" Harrison asked, but it sounded more like a statement.

"Marcus gave it to me when he went off on that gay cruise last summer. He wanted me to keep an eye on the contractors while he was gone," Justus explained.

He slipped the key into the lock and gave it a turn. It clicked and they were in.

"Marcus?" Justus called out. "It's Harrison and me, Justus."

Justus looked to the left of the foyer at the living room. Marcus leaned toward minimalism with his choices in décor. Even though the room was large, there was only a sofa that was slightly larger than a love seat, two glass-topped side tables, and a chair placed around a shaggy white area rug. The walls, painted an antique parchment color, were bare except for a single, large framed poster of a Harlequin clown that hung across from the entry.

"Marcus?" Justus called again and headed for the kitchen

door at the end of the foyer. He pushed the swinging door open and looked inside. Everything was in its place. The marbled-quartz countertops were clean and bare. There were no dishes in the sink.

Justus turned around and bumped into Harrison.

"He's not there. Maybe he's upstairs."

Harrison stepped back out of the way to let Justus pass.

"Should we be doing this?" he asked, following Justus to the foot of the stairs.

"Why not? We're his friends. We're worried about him," Justus said and started up the stairs.

"Yeah, but from what I know of him, he tends to be a little OCD when it comes to his privacy and home. He wouldn't want us going through—"

Justus turned around when Harrison suddenly stopped midsentence. He looked at the expression on Harrison's face and was not sure what he thought. "What's the matter?"

"Do you smell that?"

"Smell what?" Justus asked and took a deep breath. "I don't smell anything."

Harrison rushed up the stairs and quickly started opening doors. The two doors directly across from the staircase were the bathroom and a linen closet. The door to the right, toward the back of the house, was a bedroom-turned-office.

Justus watched him, confused. A moment ago he had the impression Harrison wanted them to leave; now he was racing around checking every door.

"What's wrong?" he asked.

Harrison opened the last door, the door to the left of the stairs at the front of the house. He stepped into the room and stopped. "Oh my god!"

Justus felt his pulse begin to race. He rushed up behind

Harrison and nearly pushed him deeper into Marcus' bedroom.

"Wha—oh my God!" he screamed. "Marcus!"

Marcus lay on his bed, with a pale-blue satin sheet twisted around his waist that left his torso and legs bare. There was a sickly yellowish hue to his skin. His head and shoulders hung lifelessly over the edge of the bed. His once beautiful blue eyes were clouded and gray, staring blindly at nothing.

"Don't touch anything," Harrison said, grabbing Justus by the arm.

"I only want to cover him up," Justus protested, tears beginning to cloud his vision. "We need to cover him."

"No. We have to get the police." Harrison's words were soft and gentle, but all Justus heard was the sharp tone of his father.

"Why?" Justus snapped and pulled his arm free.

"Because they need to see what we do," Harrison explained. "In case this was—"

Again, Harrison stopped himself. Justus stared at him while he pulled out his cell phone and walked back onto the landing.

Murder? Justus' mind filled in the blank. He turned back to Marcus. Marcus' blonde hair was disheveled and matted in places. Dried vomit crusted his mouth and stained the area rug beneath the bed.

"Marcus," he groaned. Uniformed men coming into Marcus' bedroom had been one of Marcus' biggest fantasies. The thought of them seeing him in this state caused Justus' hands to tremble. He wanted to put Marcus back in bed, untangle the sheets and make it look as if he were asleep, but Harrison's words restrained him. Tears streamed down his cheeks. He turned away.

Everything about the room appeared to be normal.

Marcus' shirt was draped over the back of the dressing chair in front of the window nearest the closet. His jeans were neatly folded and lay on the seat of the chair. Two shoes—

"That's odd," Justus murmured and wiped the tears from his eyes to get a better look. Beneath the chair sat a pair of mismatched shoes, one black Nike running shoe and one larger brown Adidas tennis shoe. Justus turned around and took a closer look at the bedroom.

"The police are on their way," Harrison said, stepping back into the room. "We should wait for them downstairs."

"You go ahead. I need a minute," Justus said.

"Okay, but really, Justus, do not touch anything."

Justus waited for Harrison to leave before he turned back around to his friend. "Oh Marcus," he said quietly. "What happened?"

Justus looked at Marcus' outstretched arm that hung over the edge of the bed. He looked at the floor and saw a small, brown bottle. It lay on the floor under the edge of the nightstand. *It must have rolled there when Marcus dropped it.* Justus picked it up and turned it over to read the label but it had been torn off. It did not matter, Justus knew what it was.

The sound of cars coming to a stop on the street below caused Justus to start. He dropped the vial and rushed back down the stairs.

Two policemen walked up on the porch. Justus let Harrison take the lead. He listened while Harrison told the police how they had come to check on their friend and what they found.

"And you have a key," the officer said and eyed Justus.

"Yes, he was my friend."

The policeman asked for everyone's name and scribbled it in a small notebook he carried before he asked Harrison to show him where the body was located.

Justus wrapped his arms around himself while tears pressed against his eyes. "Don't cry," he heard his mother's voice. "Boys don't cry, especially in public." Still one tear, followed by another and another, escaped.

Curious neighbors came out of their houses and gathered across the narrow street in front of Marcus' house. One brave boy on a bicycle, who looked to be about fifteen, tops, rolled up to the gate. Justus stared at him. In the dimming evening light, the boy resembled Marcus, with light blonde hair, blue eyes, and a gentle face.

"Did something happen to Marcus?" he asked, his voice quivered and sounded fearful.

Justus did not answer. Seeing the pained expression on the young boy's face caused his throat to tighten and choke his words.

The boy must have understood. His face contorted slightly. He looked back at the cluster of neighbors and then at the house. Tears had begun to dampen his cheeks. For a moment Justus thought the boy was about to rush up the walk and into the house. Justus looked at the boy's feet. *Too small. Thank heaven.* Suddenly, without a word, the boy turned around and pedaled away as fast as he could.

Strange.

"Justus," Harrison said, standing right outside the front door with one of the officers beside him.

Justus looked at him.

"What?"

"The officer wants to know if Marcus had any medical issues?" Harrison asked.

"No, not that I know of," Justus's voice sounded more like a raspy whisper. "Except for getting tested each year, he never saw a doctor."

"Tested?" the officer asked.

Justus looked him over. Under different circumstances, the officer was totally Justus' type. He was the butch-daddy type with touches of gray in his short dark hair, a nice neatly trimmed beard, and an athletic V shape body with the broad shoulders and small waist that guys spent decades in the gym to achieve.

"HIV testing," Justus answered.

"Oh," the officer said and made a note in his book. "We found this." He held up the empty bottle. "Do you have any idea what was in it?"

Justus felt his heart skip. He glanced at Harrison before looking back at the officer. "Poppers," he answered and noticed the officer's confused expression. "Rush. Amyl. Some guys use it in the club and when having sex to get a bit of a high."

"I know what it is," he said in a judgmental tone. Instantly, he changed from hot to not in Justus' mind. "I've radioed for the coroner to come and collect the body," the officer continued in the same tone. "Is there any next of kin we should notify?"

"Justus?" Harrison asked when he did not answer.

"No," Justus shook his head. "He has no one, only me."

"Is there someone he authorized to make his final arrangements?"

"He has a will in the file cabinet in the den."

"Den?" the officer asked.

"The other room at the top of the stairs," Justus said slowly, as though talking to a child.

"Okay," the officer said, sounding a bit puzzled. "It might be better if you got it for me."

"Sure," Justus answered.

He walked back into the house and headed up the stairs.

Two officers stood in the doorway of Marcus' bedroom talking in low voices. Justus instantly disliked them but resisted the urge to snap at them. He turned toward the second bedroom and walked over to the file cabinet beside the window that overlooked the backyard. He pulled the top drawer open and found the red folder in the back with the label Important Papers. He pulled the file out and turned around, nearly bumping into the officer.

"Here," Justus said and held out the papers.

"Thank you," the officer said in a gentle tone. "I'm really sorry about your friend."

Justus closed the file drawer while he looked at the officer. *Nope. Still a jerk.*

Back on the front porch, the reality of what happened began to set in as the sun dropped out of sight and the streetlights flickered on. Justus turned away from the officer and Harrison, retreating to the far corner of the front porch. In the shadows, he wrapped his arms around himself as he began to cry quietly.

"The police say we can go now," Harrison said, putting his hands on Justus' quivering shoulders.

"No," Justus answered. He shook his head and tried to collect himself. "No. I want to stay until they take him away."

"Are you sure?" Harrison asked.

"Yes." Justus nodded. He wiped his damp cheeks with his hands and then dried his hands on his jeans. He took a deep breath and managed to hold back his tears. He turned around. When Harrison slipped his arm around him, Justus leaned into him.

The officer held out the folder to Justus. "It says you're the executor of your friend's estate. You'll need this."

Suddenly the memory of their talk a few weeks ago rushed back, filling Justus' head. He looked at Harrison. "Will you help me?"

"Of course," Harrison answered and gave Justus a one-armed hug.

The sound of a car approaching caused Justus to look at the street. The crowd across the street had grown. Justus spotted the boy on his bike. He had returned but stayed away from the others as he sat staring at the house. A black Ford van pulled to a stop in the middle of the street and blocked Justus' view of the boy.

Two men jumped out of the van. The driver met the passenger at the rear doors. They pulled a gurney out and wheeled it through the gate and up the walk. When they reached the steps, they lifted it to the porch and took it through the front door.

The whole scene reminded Justus of the detective shows he had seen on TV. The two men with the gurney were dressed in black with white lab coats. One carried a clipboard, the other a camera. In his mind he could see the man with the camera taking pictures of Marcus and his bedroom. *Marcus would have hated that.* They would put Marcus' body on the gurney, cover it with a white sheet, and then wheel him away.

Justus heard some talking in the foyer inside. He looked at the door. There was the sound of metal squealing, and then one of the men backed out onto the porch, pulling the gurney. Justus' breath caught when he saw the heavy, black-plastic zippered bag on the gurney. He knew Marcus' body was inside. The rush of reality hit him again, like a punch in the gut. He gasped and wrapped his arms around himself. He felt Harrison's arm pull him closer, steadying him. Tears once again blurred his vision while he watched the men take Marcus away.

The officer came back out and stood in front of them.

"One question before you leave, do you know who he

was with?" he asked.

"No," Justus answered.

"What makes you think he was with someone?" Harrison asked.

"He was still wearing a condom."

"Oh, dear God," Justus gasped. Tears began to stream down his cheeks. He felt sick over the humiliation of it all. *Why wouldn't Harrison let me clean him up? Marcus deserved better than this.* He turned toward Harrison. "Get me out of here, please."

"It's okay. We're done here," the policeman said.

One of the other officers walked out onto the porch. He held several plastic bags that resembled large, zip-lock storage bags. Inside one was the brown vial; another, the condom. Justus looked away afraid to see what other items they had collected from Marcus' private bedroom.

"If you have any questions, here's my card." The officer handed Harrison the card. "We'll be in touch."

"Thank you," Harrison said.

Justus dried his tears. He watched the policemen walk back to their cars.

"I want to take a look inside before we go," he said. "Make sure they didn't trash the place."

"They wouldn't do that," Harrison said.

"I still want to look."

They made a quick tour of the house. Everything was as they had found it except for Marcus' bedroom. The bedsheets had been stripped, bundled up, and left in the center of the bed as though it were laundry day. Justus looked in the closet. Everything was in its place. The shoes beneath the chair were gone as were the clothes.

"Ready?" Harrison asked.

Justus nodded.

Walking back out onto the front porch, Harrison locked the front door and made sure it was secure. While he headed for the car, Justus glanced across the street. The crowd had dispersed. The boy on his bike was gone. Everything seemed quiet and normal again.

CHAPTER THIRTEEN

Justus woke up still tired and feeling as if he had been beaten up. His eyes felt puffy and scratchy, and his chest hurt inside. Slowly he pushed himself up and sat with his feet on the cold wooden floor of his bedroom.

Was it all a dream? Please, let it have been a bad dream.

He heard voices downstairs.

What time is it? He looked at his alarm clock. It was nearly one in the afternoon.

What day is it? He thought hard but still was not quite sure.

Slowly he made his way out to the hall and down the stairs.

Scotty sat in the living room curled up on the couch. His eyes were red and his cheeks damp with tears. He stared at nothing, seemingly lost in his thoughts.

Dale sat at the other end of the sofa. He looked up when Justus walked into the room.

"When did you get here?" Justus asked. His voice cracked.

"About ten, right after Harrison called," Dale answered in a somber tone.

"Harry called you?"

"Yeah."

Justus noticed the two glasses on the coffee table. *Harrison must have poured them a drink.*

"What time is it?" he asked.

"It's a little after one."

Justus looked around the room and could not focus. His head felt numb, as though he had been drinking.

"Where's Harry?"

"He's in the kitchen with Doug," Dale answered.

Justus looked at Scotty before he turned around and headed to the kitchen.

"I don't know," Harrison was saying to Douglas when Justus walked into the room. "You're up."

Justus did not answer. He stared at the coffee pot and then at the glass of wine on the island. Something brushed against his leg. He looked down. Col. Mustard rubbed himself against Justus and looked up at him. He mewed.

"Come here," Douglas said and stood up. He wrapped his arms around Justus and gave him a hug. "I'm so sorry," he said into his ear.

Justus grabbed Douglas and held onto him. Tears filled his eyes and overflowed. He buried his face in Douglas' chest and cried.

"It's going to be okay," Douglas whispered and held him tighter. "You'll get through this. We'll help you."

It took a while but Justus finally regained a bit of composure. He loosened his hold on Douglas and stepped back.

Douglas' shirt was damp with tears. Justus reached up and tried to wipe it dry.

"It's okay," Douglas said in a gentle tone. "What would you like to drink?"

"Do we have any Jack Daniel's?"

"Whiskey?" Harrison asked and gave him a surprised look. "How about some coffee first?"

"Only if it has something stronger than cream in it," Justus answered.

"How about I make you something," Douglas spoke up and walked around to the other side of the island. He opened the cupboard in the island and bent down. "Let's see what you have down here," he mumbled. "Aha! Perfect." He grabbed three bottles and put them on the counter behind him. He closed the cabinet with his foot.

Justus looked at the countertop, at the dark gray veins that gave it that Carrara marble look. He mindlessly followed a vein to the edge where it stopped.

"Here you go," Douglas said and turned around. He slid a mug of what appeared to be black coffee across the island.

"What is it?" Justus asked.

"Just taste it."

Hesitantly Justus raised the mug to his lips. He inhaled the aroma and smelled the presence of alcohol. He looked at Douglas who stood leaning against the island with his palms pressed flat against the countertop. He was watching Justus intently.

Justus took a sip and let the warm brew linger in his mouth. He could taste Kahlua and chocolate. It was not bad.

"Sorry there was no whipped cream," Douglas said. "It's better with a dab."

"This is really good," Justus finally said after he

swallowed. "What is it?"

"It's called a coffee nudge."

"I think I found my new favorite drink."

Douglas smiled.

"Lunch will be ready soon," Harrison said. "Are you hungry?"

Justus thought for a moment. He was not sure. He took a deep breath and realized he smelled a pot roast cooking in the oven. He looked at the stove and saw a steaming pot. Looking back at Harrison, he shrugged.

"I should check on Dale and Scotty," Douglas said and left the room.

"Are you still tired?" Harrison asked.

"I don't know," Justus answered. "I just feel strange."

"That's to be expected. It was quite a shock."

"How's Scotty? You didn't tell him how we found Marcus did you?"

"I only said we found him in his bed."

Justus nodded and took another sip. "Good. Marcus wouldn't want him to know the details." He suddenly remembered something and looked around the kitchen. "Where's the folder?"

"It's right where you left it, by the phone," Harrison answered and motioned toward the counter against the wall behind Justus.

Justus turned to see. Harrison was right. It was beside the telephone, only he could not remember putting it there.

"Why don't you go take a shower, it might help?"

"Yeah, I guess," Justus answered.

"Lunch will be ready when you finish."

Justus stood up. He took his drink and headed for his bathroom upstairs.

The hot water felt good against Justus' neck and shoulders. He rolled his head back and forth letting the jets in the showerhead massage the tightness away. He tilted his head back and let the water run through his hair and down this face, washing away the images in his head. Turning around, he readjusted the nozzle to a rain setting and was drenched in warmth. Slowly the numbness drained away leaving fresh, raw pain that stung.

Justus' legs gave under the weight of his grief and he crumpled onto the floor of the shower. He wrapped his arms around his legs and buried his face in his knees while the water continued to rain down on him, drowning his sobs.

When he returned downstairs, everyone was seated at the table in the dining room. Justus set his empty coffee mug down beside his plate.

"Another?" Douglas asked. He reached across the table in front of Scotty and picked up the mug.

"Please," Justus answered and pulled out his chair. He glanced at Harrison seated across from him while he sat down. "Smells wonderful," he said in an attempt to get back some sense of normal. He looked to his right, at Dale seated in front of the large, leaded-glass window. Then to his left at Scotty, who was seated beside Douglas' empty chair. Scotty had the same blank stare he had earlier. He sat with his hands resting on either side of the plate in front of him. Justus reached over and gave his hand a squeeze. Scotty looked at him. His eyes were wet, blood shot, and lost. "We'll be okay," Justus whispered. Scotty nodded.

Douglas returned and set Justus' steaming cup on the table in front of him.

"Thank you," Justus said.

Douglas looked around the table. "Anyone need another drink while I'm up?" No one responded. "Okay," Douglas said and sat back down.

Harrison put several chunks of pot roast onto his plate, followed by carrots and small red potatoes. Justus watched. Douglas helped himself to the fresh rolls while he waited for the roast plater. Justus watched in silence. Neither Scotty nor Dale made any motion toward the food.

"Come on, guys, eat," Harrison urged. He looked at Dale. "There more Jack if you'd like."

Justus inhaled sharply at the sound of Jack's name. He looked at Dale and Scotty before looking at Harrison. He watched Harrison's expression change to a shocked look.

"I'm so sorry," he apologized. "I meant Jack Daniel's."

"It's okay," Justus said, feeling his strength returning. "With everything—I had forgotten about Jack. We have to find him now more than ever." He looked at Dale again. "Are you doing okay?"

"Yeah," he answered in a weak voice.

Justus looked at Scotty. "Scotty," he said and put his hand over Scotty's again.

Slowly, Scotty turned and looked at Justus. He opened his mouth but no sound came out.

Justus felt his own throat tighten. He gave a sympathetic smile. He wanted to tell him that Marcus loved him, but knew it would send Scotty even deeper into his grief.

"Please, eat something," Justus said.

Scotty did not react. He turned his head and looked down at his plate while Douglas put a spoonful of pot roast and potatoes on it.

After several attempts at conversation, the five fell into

silence and tried to eat. Justus took a bite. The roast tasted wonderful but when he tried to swallow it, it felt as if it stuck in his throat. He took a drink of water.

"How about some music?" Douglas suggested.

"Sure," Harrison said. He jumped up and went into the living room where his vinyl record collection and stereo were. Justus looked over his shoulder to see which album Harrison would choose. From his seat at the table, he could not see but a moment later the house came alive with the sound of Stevie Nicks' voice.

Rumors. 1977. Justus recognized the album.

Lunch was over by the time Side A finished playing. Scotty scarcely touched his food even with Douglas' encouragement. Dale managed a bite and then seemed to snap back to normal and finished his plateful, even having a second.

The five left the table and went into the living room. They listened to Side B while they had another round of drinks.

"I think I should go on home," Dale said when he finished his drink.

"You don't have to go," Harrison said. "You could stay the night."

"No," Dale answered. "Thank you but I think I need to be home."

"Okay," Harrison answered.

Everyone but Scotty stood up and gave Dale a hug. Afterward, Harrison and Douglas retreated to the kitchen to put the leftovers away and clean up.

Justus walked Dale to the front door. "Are you sure you have to go?"

"Yes," Dale answered. "I have to. Seeing Scotty like this, I can't stop thinking about Jack. I don't know what I would do if—We have to find him. He has to be okay."

"I know. We will." Justus gave his friend a hug and watched him head down the walk to his car parked by the curb. Once Dale drove away, he closed the door and returned to the living room. He sat down beside Scotty. He put his hands between his knees but really wanted to put his arm around his friend.

"I–I," Scotty stammered. "I was in love with him, you know."

"Yes," Justus answered.

Tears dampened Scotty's red cheeks again. "Every time he walked into the room, my heart would beat faster. Every time he left with another man, I died a little inside, but I still loved him and hoped that one day he would notice me."

Justus nodded to himself. "I'm sure he did."

"No," Scotty said and shook his head. "Don't pretend for me. I do that enough already. He never had a clue; and now, he'll never know."

Justus turned and started to hug him but Scotty put his hand up.

"Please, don't. I'm trying to hold on. If you hug me—I don't want to fall apart."

"I understand," Justus said and sat back. "I love you, Scotty."

"Me, too."

"Would you like some more Coke?" Justus asked, seeing Scotty's empty glass sitting on the coffee table.

"No, I'm fine for now, thank you."

"Okay. I'll be back."

He stood up and headed to the kitchen. The knot in his chest from trying to suppress his emotions made his heart ache. He barely reached the dining room before tears blurred his vision. He stumbled into the kitchen.

Harrison and Douglas sat across from each other at the island. Harrison sipped on his glass of red wine while Douglas drank his beer from the bottle. They stopped talking when Justus came into the room. Douglas jumped up and wrapped his arms around Justus.

"It's okay," he said.

Justus once again was overcome by his grief and gave way to tears. His sobs were muffled by Douglas' chest.

"Would you like another drink?" Harrison offered when Justus pulled away from Douglas' hug.

Justus nodded.

"I'll make it," Douglas said.

Justus sat down. "So now what?"

"What do you mean?" Harrison asked.

"What do I do now? Who arranges for the funeral?"

"Well, you do."

"Me?"

"Yes, as his executor it's left up to you. But Doug and I will help you with whatever you need. Won't we?"

"You bet," Douglas answered when he handed Justus his drink.

"Thank you," Justus said and set the mug down. "I have no idea what I'm supposed to do or what Marcus wanted."

"Have you looked at the will?"

"No. I can't right now," Justus admitted. He looked behind him at the counter. The manila file folder sat next to the telephone.

"May I?" Harrison asked.

"Be my guest," Justus answered.

Harrison walked around the island and picked up the folder. He returned to his stool and sat down. Opening the folder, he appeared to scan the papers.

Justus watched him and took a drink from his mug.

"It says here that Marcus wanted to be cremated and his ashes are to be buried in a cemetery to be determined later."

"Cremated? How do I do that?"

"You don't. The mortuary does it all," Douglas answered.

"Oh." Justus looked at the dark liquid in his mug. He watched the tiny ripples move across the surface while he wrapped his hands around the sides of the cup. "When do we have to do that?"

"Tomorrow we can check to see when the coroner will release his body, and then we can find a mortuary. Don't worry about the financial part yet, I'll take care of it and we can settle up when we find out if he has any money in the estate," Harrison answered.

Justus nodded. Even though he could rely on Harrison and Douglas for help, he still felt overwhelmed.

Harrison closed the folder and left it sitting in the middle of the island.

CHAPTER FOURTEEN

Rain poured down while Harrison parked the Honda CR-V in the driveway. Justus sat in the passenger seat, his arms wrapped around a polished wooden box. He stared at the dashboard.

His ears kept ringing with the words of the coroner.

Your friend died from a cardiac arrhythmia. There were traces of amyl nitrate but whether or not it was a contributing factor was inconclusive. His medical records reported he had coronary artery disease. So using it at all was risky for him. In fact, it's risky for anyone to use it.

"Are you okay?" Harrison asked and put his hand on Justus' arm. "You haven't said a thing all the way home."

Justus heard the words but it took a while for them to register. He forced himself to look away from the latch on the glovebox. He looked at Harrison.

"Yeah, I'm okay," he answered even though he knew inside he was not. He looked at the box on his lap. It was hard for him to imagine that it contained what was left of his friend, reduced to ashes.

"Come on," Harrison said, breaking the silence. "Let's get inside. I know someone who could use a drink and you probably could use one as well."

Justus sat for a moment, unable to move. Finally, he forced one of his hands to let go of the box long enough to open the door. He stepped out of the car and protectively hunched over the box to shield it from the rain. He closed the car door and made a run for the backdoor.

Inside, Harrison was already pouring them a drink, a glass of wine for himself and a glass of something stronger for Justus. Justus walked over to the counter by the phone and hesitated a moment before finally setting the box down. He returned to the island in the middle of the kitchen and pulled a stool out from under the ledge. Harrison slid the glass across the marble countertop.

"So, do you know what you are going to do with the ashes yet?" Harrison asked.

"No," Justus answered and took a sip of his drink.

"Maybe the guys can help you decide."

"Yeah," Justus agreed.

"I know it's not Friday, but why don't you give them a call and go have a drink with them?"

"I'm not really in the mood," he answered and took another sip from his glass. Whatever it was that Harrison had poured for him burned his throat.

"Nonsense," Harrison said. "You haven't been out of the house for a week except to deal with this." He motioned at the wooden box across the room. "You need to get out among the living again and have some fun. All of you need to."

"I don't know."

"Hey, Marcus wouldn't want you all to wither up and hide away. He'd want you to get out there and enjoy life."

Justus did not look up from his glass. Deep down he knew Harrison was right. Still he felt numb inside and all he wanted to do was crawl in a corner and disappear.

"I can't," he finally said and shook his head before slugging back the last of his drink.

"I know everything seems pointless and like nothing will ever be the same as it was," Harrison said while he pulled out the other stool and sat down at the end of the island. "But trust me on this, it will get better but you have to try."

"I've never known anyone who died. I mean, sure I knew my grandparents but they were old, they weren't young."

"I know," Harrison answered.

"How did you go on after your parents died?"

"I don't know. I just did. I would wake up every morning and all I wanted to do was roll over and give up, but then I thought about Dani. Her life was ripped apart too. She needed me to be strong. So I forced myself to get out of bed and even though it felt like I was going through the motions, I kept living. In time it got easier and I started feeling again.

"Justus, Dale, and especially Scotty need you now. Be strong for them."

Justus let Harrison's words sink in. What Harrison had described was exactly how he felt, hollow and empty inside like a chocolate Easter rabbit. He glanced at the calendar on the wall beside the hall archway. The Easter party was Saturday, only a week away. The tickets had already been bought. If the gang was going to make it to the party, they should venture out before then. He looked at Harrison.

"So, does that mean you'll come too?"

"I can't tonight," he answered, sounding disappointed

though Justus knew it was an act. "Doug is coming over. We're going to watch some TV and have a pizza."

"Sounds like a date," Justus said without hesitation.

"It's not a date," Harrison said dryly.

Justus saw Harrison's jaw tighten slightly which made him smile inside.

"Oh, it's simply dinner and a movie," he said and nodded, not even trying to hide the sarcasm in his tone.

Harrison opened his mouth to speak but nothing came out. He closed his mouth and pursed his lips. "It's not a date," he answered firmly and stood up. "Go call the guys."

Justus smiled. He stood up, slid the stool back under the island's ledge. He walked over to Harrison.

"I love you," he said and wrapped his arms around Harrison. He felt Harrison's body tense for a moment and then his arms return the hug. Justus held the embrace just long enough to feel Harrison become uncomfortable. He let go and headed for the stairs. When he reached the archway to the dining room he thought he heard Harrison whisper, "I love you back." Justus smiled and kept walking.

It took a lot of begging and several phone calls back and forth, but Justus and Dale finally convinced Scotty to join them at Stumptown. The music was loud and thumping as normal. Dale was already seated at their usual table when Justus walked through the door. He made a quick stop at the bar to grab a drink before he headed across the semi-crowded dance floor to his table.

"Any sign of him?" he asked while he sat down.

"Not yet, but I texted him and he said he's on his way." Dale answered.

"Good."

"So, how've you been?" Dale asked.

"Okay." Justus felt his mood start to sink. "Let's not talk about this. I wanna have some fun tonight."

"Okay," Dale agreed. "Sorry."

"It's fine." Justus took a sip of his drink.

"Hey, that's not rum and Coke!" Dale nearly shouted when he saw the contents of Justus' glass.

"No. It's Jack Daniel's."

"Wow, and I thought I was the wild one of the bunch."

"No, you're a bad influence," Justus teased. "Hey, he's here."

Scotty had his head ducked down and his hands stuffed into the pockets of his jacket. The two watched him make his way around the edge of the dance floor to the table.

"You made it!" Justus said and gave Scotty a hug.

Scotty did not hug him back. He pulled out the chair between the two guys and sat down, keeping his hands in his pockets.

"You doing okay?" Dale asked and looked concerned.

Scotty did not look good. It had only been four days since he learned the news about Marcus, but he already looked as if he had lost weight. His face seemed thinner. There were dark circles around his eyes. He nodded his response.

"I'm glad you're here," Justus told him. "We need to get back to normal."

Scotty looked at him. "Normal?" he said in a raspy voice, unlike his normal cheery pitch. "We'll never be normal. First Jack, now Marcus."

"Well, hi there," the shirtless server greeted them, interrupting. "I haven't seen you guys in weeks. Where have you been?"

"We've been checking out CC's," Justus answered

before either Dale or Scotty said something to bring everyone down.

The server pulled back a bit and eyed them. "Checking out the competition?"

"There is no competition," Justus assured him. "This is the only real club in town."

"Glad to hear it. So, what are we drinking tonight?"

"I'll have another appletini," Dale ordered.

"Oh, good choice, Mario is fabulous at making those. How about you?"

Justus drank down the rest of his Jack Daniel's a little too quickly. It burned all the way down, but he was determined not to let on to the others. "I'll have another Jack Daniel's on ice. Make it a double, please."

"Okay?" the server eyed him curiously and then turned a bit to look at Scotty. "A Coke for you?"

"No," Scotty spoke up. "I'll have what he's having."

"A Jack Daniel's?" the server said, his tone registering the shock that was reflected on both Dale's and Justus' faces.

"Yes," Scotty said firmly.

"All righty then, be back in a flash." The server disappeared in the crowd.

"A Jack Daniel's?" Justus and Dale said in unison.

Scotty looked at them. "What? This is a bar and I'm over twenty-one."

"Yeah, but you don't drink," Dale said.

"Well, the people I love aren't supposed to drop like flies either."

Justus looked at Dale to see his reaction to what Scotty had just said, but there was none. It was as if Scotty's public confession was old news. Justus put his hand over Scotty's and gave it a gentle squeeze.

"You're right," Justus said and nodded in agreement. "So, let's enjoy the music and the scenery, okay?"

"Fine with me," Scotty said.

Justus glanced at Dale who sat looking confused yet concerned.

The music was great. The DJ had put together a lineup of retro-disco and dance music from when Stumptown first opened. The server called it Flashback Friday. Justus was in heaven. He loved the music and it was the perfect thing to lift him out of his funk. Justus' enthusiasm, or perhaps the liquor, elevated Scotty's woe-is-me mood. He stood beside Justus at the edge of the dance floor and bopped in time with the music.

Justus took another sip of his third Jack Daniel's of the night and looked across the dance floor. A handsome man with light-colored hair, a nice smile, and a killer bod was looking at him. Justus felt a stirring inside. *Just what the doctor ordered.* The man started to make his way over to him. Justus felt the excitement of anticipation bubbling inside him. He smiled and watched the man make his approach. Justus took a quick sip of his drink to wet his dry mouth.

"Hi," the man said in a wonderfully deep, masculine voice and held out his hand to Scotty. "My name is Aaron."

"Scotty." Scotty took his hand and Justus' heart sank.

"I was watching you and thought you might like to dance?" Aaron continued.

"Sure," Scotty said. He gulped down the last of his drink and handed the glass to Justus before letting Aaron lead him to the center of the dance floor.

"Wow!" Dale said when he took Scotty's place beside Justus. "Our little boy has grown up right before our eyes," he said in a fake, teary voice.

"Not funny," Justus answered and returned to their table.

Dale followed.

The server came rushing over to them. "Have you heard?" he asked.

Justus and Dale exchanged confused looks.

"Heard what?" Dale asked first.

"Another person has gone missing," the server answered in a melodramatic tone.

"Missing? Who?" Justus asked. He felt his heart pound faster, silently hoping he would not say Marcus' name.

"A guy named Barry."

Justus' breath caught. The image of Barry talking with Dean flashed in his mind so vividly he thought it was real.

"What?" he nearly shouted. "When?"

"The last anyone saw him was at the party we had last month."

"The Saint Paddy's Day Bash?" Dale asked.

"Yep."

"But we were here that night," Dale said. "I don't remember seeing anything." He looked at Justus and his eyes widened.

"Does anyone know what happened?" Justus asked. His hands trembled when he started to raise his glass to his lips. He quickly put it back down on the table.

"Someone said they saw him leave with an older gentleman."

"Were they arguing?"

"No, I don't think so. The guy said they were practically making out."

Justus felt confused. When he had seen Dean talking to Barry, they had been far from making out. In fact, Dean had looked as though he had been ready to punch Barry.

"That makes four," Dale said. "Alexander from Embers,

Cody from CC's, Jack and now Barry from here."

"Crazy isn't it," the server said. "I better make my rounds. Can I get you another?"

"Sure," they both answered.

Once the server was gone, Dale leaned across the table. "What was that about?" he asked, glancing at Justus' hands gripping the glass.

"I think I know who Barry was with," Justus answered.

Dale looked surprised. "You do?"

"Yes. I saw Dean talking to Barry that night. They were standing at the end of the bar. Only, they didn't look like they were making out. More like Dean was ready to fight him."

"Did they leave together?"

"I don't know. I slipped out first. That's the night Scotty went off with that Andy guy who bought him a drink. Only when I was leaving, I ran into the jerk coming back in."

"Have you heard back from that Curtis guy about the picture?"

"No." Justus shook his head. He tried to take a drink again but his hand continued to tremble, rattling the ice cubes against the sides of the glass. He put it back on the table before he splashed it on everything and everyone.

"Oh my God!" Dale gasped.

"What?" Justus looked at him.

Dale was looking at the dance floor with wide-eyed shock. Justus turned to see for himself. His jaw dropped. In the center of the dance floor Scotty and Aaron were locked in an embrace, kissing like lovers.

It was two in the morning when Justus walked into the house. A night out had sounded like a good idea but it had quickly turned into one surprise after another. The image of

Scotty and Aaron making out on the dance floor and the voice of the server telling them that Barry had disappeared kept running through his head, making him dizzy, or was it the alcohol?

"Have a good time?"

Justus jumped and spun around, the front door nearly slamming shut. "Don't sneak up on people," he snapped. "You could give them a heart attack."

"I wasn't sneaking. I was getting a glass of water."

Justus looked at Harrison and realized he was standing in the middle of the dining room wearing a pair of sleeping shorts holding a glass. "Oh," he said. "Where's Doug, in bed?"

"If you must know," Harrison answered back.

Justus felt his jaw drop. "Really?" he gasped, suddenly sober.

"No!" Harrison answered with a laugh followed by a disapproving crease that formed between his eyebrows. "I've told you, he has a lady friend and besides, we are not gay."

"Keep telling yourselves that," Justus teased.

"So how was your evening?" Harrison asked.

"It was eye opening, to say the least." Justus' head began to throb and he needed to sit down. He walked over to the dining room table and sat down in his usual chair.

"Really? How so?" Harrison looked confused. He pulled out a chair and sat down.

"For starters, Scotty now drinks in public. He also makes out with strange men in the middle of the dance floor."

"Really?"

"Yep. But there's more. He admitted that he loves, loved Marcus."

Harrison did not comment. He simply nodded and looked at his water glass.

"There's more."

"More?"

"Another man has gone missing and this time I'm positive I know who is behind it."

"What?" Harrison's tone reflected his shock. "Who?"

"Dean."

CHAPTER FIFTEEN

Monday had become the new Friday, at least that was how Justus felt. He dreaded weekends the way most people did Mondays. Weekends had become the time bad news was shared, destroying any hope for fun.

Ever since hearing the news about Barry's disappearance, Justus could not get him off his mind. They had only shared an hour or so, but in that short time Justus had learned enough to know he did not want any harm to come to him. Still, he could not shake the feeling that something had happened to him and that Dean was behind it.

The elevator stopped and the doors opened on the twenty-eighth floor. Justus waited for Harrison to exit before he followed.

"Try to have a good day," Harrison said and smiled while they walked.

"Easier said than done," Justus answered.

Vicki was waiting for him outside the file room.

"Please don't tell me there's another vase of flowers," he groaned.

"Afraid so," she answered.

"I hope you kept them. I really don't want to see them."

"I thought you would say that," she smiled. "I hope you keep this guy around, a girl could get spoiled," she lowered her tone to a naughty pitch, "and I want to be spoiled." Her voice raised again. "Here's the card, you should at least read it."

"Why? Did you?" Justus took the yellow envelope she held out to him.

"I refuse to answer that on the grounds. . . uh, I don't remember the rest, but you know." She shrugged her shoulders coyly.

"You're so bad!" Justus teased. He stuck the envelope into the folder.

"Since when do you bring work home?" she asked upon seeing the file in his hands.

"This isn't work stuff," he said. "A friend of mine named me executor of his will. I've been putting off reading it completely and Harry—Mr. Andrews said I need to. So. . ." He frowned and held up the folder, surrendering to it.

"I'm sorry," Vicki commiserated. "I should get back to the mail room. If you need anything, call me."

"I will, thanks," Justus said to be polite and went into the file room.

The florescent lights, connected to a motion sensor, flickered to life. Justus walked over to his desk and tossed the folder into his in-basket. He opened the top drawer and pulled out his Broadway Hits CD and popped it into the player.

While the Phantom sang to Christine, Justus emptied his cart of the files. He spread them out on the empty desk and began to sort them, putting them in numerical order. The

Phantom's baritone voice resonated and filled the room. Justus felt his shoulders and neck relax while he became lost in the music and sang along. His back was toward the doorway when he and the Phantom reached the climax in the song.

"I didn't know you could sing."

Justus let out a scream and spun around, the file in his hand sent its contents raining down on the floor around him.

"Harry!" he spat. "Don't sneak up on people! You could give them a heart attack. And stop laughing, it's rude."

"I'm sorry," Harrison apologized, but his continued laughter said otherwise.

"What do you want?" Justus asked and knelt down by his desk to begin picking up the papers.

"I hope that wasn't one of mine," Harrison said. He stooped down and began helping Justus.

"It would serve you right," Justus snapped.

Together they gathered the papers and Justus put them back in the folder.

"I'll put it in order for you," Harrison volunteered.

"Thanks," Justus said and handed him the file. "So, what did you want?"

"Oh!" Harrison gasped. "I have a meeting with the Concannon Industries rep and I need their files."

"Okay, when do you need them?"

"Now," Harrison said and grimaced.

"Now? Harry, I—I'll get them and bring them to you. Where is your meeting?"

"In Conference Room Three upstairs."

"Fine. I'll bring them up."

"Thanks," Harrison said and started to leave. "I'm sorry I startled you, and you do have a good voice," he said over his shoulder and then disappeared around the corner.

Justus pulled his chair out and sat down in front of his computer. He quickly typed in the name of the business and did a search. Every company they worked on was assigned a number. Those numbers were used to mark their files. It was not the best system since every time one of the people on the floor needed a file, he would have to first look up the account number and then go to the file cabinet. If they would simply file everything under the name of the business in alphabetical order, he could go straight to the cabinet and pull the needed file.

Justus wrote down the ten-digit number and went to the file cabinet. The Concannon Industries file was right after the White's Electronic account and before the Fischel's. Justus put in a large orange card to mark the location of the missing file and closed the drawer. The marker cards had been his idea, one that his former workmate Debra had tried to claim as hers. However, when she tried to explain it to their boss and failed, she'd had to admit it was his idea after all.

Justus decided to take the stairs after seeing a small group of people from the business that shared their floor already waiting for the elevator. The stairs would be much faster.

He emerged onto the twenty-ninth floor a bit winded. He had been on this floor many times in his young career. The floor housed the company big shots and their secretaries. There were also five conference rooms where the reps from downstairs would meet with their clients. The powers that be did not want clients to see the cubicles; they wanted to keep the illusion of opulence. "Opulence breeds trust," the VP had once told them while he stood on top of a desk downstairs. The only thing Justus liked about the man was that when he stood next to the VP, Justus finally felt tall.

Conference Room Three was located on the outside east wall and had windows that overlooked the Willamette River and

Southeast Portland. On the rare clear days it even had a nice view of Mount Hood in the distance. Justus knocked lightly on the door and then slipped into the room.

Harrison sat at the head of a long polished cherrywood table. There was a white board on the wall behind him that had some figures and a chart drawn on it. Three men in suits sat stone-faced with their backs toward the windows. Justus stepped up and sat the files down on the corner of the table by Harrison's left elbow. He glanced up at the men and froze as his eyes locked on the one seated furthest away.

"Thank you, Justus."

Justus heard Harrison, but his words and their meaning did not register. His attention was fixed on the dark-haired man with a neatly trimmed mustache at the end of the table. The man fidgeted and appeared nervous, obviously recognizing Justus.

"Justus?" Harrison touched his arm. "Is everything alright?"

"Yes." Justus finally found his voice and pulled himself away from staring at the man. "Sorry, heights. Don't like 'em."

Justus turned around and slipped out of the room. Once safely in the hall he leaned against the wall and caught his breath. *What's he doing here?* He pulled out his cell phone and punched Scotty's work number in from memory then tapped send. The call rang.

"Come on, answer," he said impatiently while he headed back downstairs to the file room. The call dropped when he entered the stairwell and right when Scotty answered. "Damn it!" Justus ran down the stairs and emerged on the twenty-eighth floor. While he continued on his way to the file room, he redialed Scotty's number.

"Thank you for calling Qwik Print. This is Eugene, how may I help you?"

"Scotty, it's me, Justus."

"Justus? What's the matter?"

"You are never going to believe who's here in a meeting with Harrison."

"Okay, who?"

"Andy."

"Andy? What's he doing there?"

Justus was surprised by Scotty's tone. He had thought he would have been shocked. Instead, Scotty sounded bored.

"He was in a meeting with Harrison and the guys from Concannon Industries."

"We all have to work somewhere, I suppose."

"It was all I could do not to jump him about what he did to you—"

"Yeah, well, I gotta go, a customer just walked in."

"Okay, but why don't you come over for dinner tonight?"

"Sure, bye."

The call disconnected but Justus tapped the red dot in the center of the screen on his phone anyway. He sat down at his desk and stared at his dark computer screen. He felt restless inside, as though he had drunk the whole pot of coffee. *Coffee, that's what I need.* He jumped up and went to the break room.

Three women and a stuffy, square-jawed man sat together around a table by the counter. Justus ignored them and went to fill his coffee cup.

"Did you see the paper this morning? Another one of them has gone missing from one of those so-called nightclubs," one of the women said.

"I saw that, too," another spoke up in a slightly bored tone. "I don't understand why this is newsworthy?"

"Really," the man agreed. "Who cares? I mean, it's one

less pervert on the street."

"I agree. Yesterday my pastor gave a sermon explaining all of the vile things they do with each other and how they are an abomination and go against nature and God," the last woman at the table spat. "It's Sodom and Gomorrah all over again."

Justus felt his pulse quicken. He turned around sharply, nearly spilling his coffee. "I'm sure it's nothing you haven't done yourselves with your husbands."

"I never!" the last woman who spoke gasped.

"Yeah, right," Justus scoffed. "You probably take it in the ass every night."

"That was uncalled for," the man said. "You're talking to a lady."

"I know who I'm talking to," Justus snapped, "four homophobic, self-righteous assholes."

The man jumped to his feet. His hands were clenched into fists and looking as if he were ready for a fight.

"Struck a nerve? Gonna hit me?" Justus said and took a step closer even though inside he wanted to run. "Do it and you'll get fired."

The expression on the man's face softened a bit. It was obvious Justus' words registered.

"Those men you so easily dismissed are people too. They're some mother's little baby, some father's son. Their families are probably sick with worry over them right now. But you go ahead and keep talking your hateful trash. Your day is coming."

"What's that supposed to mean?" one woman snapped back.

"Is that a threat?" another asked.

"I think you should leave," the man ordered more than suggested.

Justus laughed. "You people are pathetic."

He walked out of the room, his pulse still pounding wildly. He did not stop until he was back in his file room. He wished his office had a door. He dropped a CD into his player and pressed the play button. While the soundtrack of the 1984 movie *Footloose* played, Justus slid down the file cabinet and sat on the floor behind his desk. He buried his face in his crossed arms. Tears dampened his face while he thought about Jack and Barry and the other missing men and how cruel people were.

"What's the matter?"

Justus looked up at Harrison standing beside his desk. He quickly dried his eyes and stood up, brushing himself off more out of habit than actually removing any dirt.

"Nothing. Nothing," he stammered.

"Well, ready for lunch?"

Justus looked up at the clock and was surprised to see it was already one in the afternoon. "Sure."

Before leaving the room, Justus turned off his CD player and looked at the neat stacks of files. He felt as though he were forgetting something but nothing came to mind. He followed Harrison to the elevators.

It did not take long for the elevator car to arrive. The doors opened and Justus entered, finding his place against the back wall. He gripped the handrail and leaned his back against the wall to keep from falling over. He hated the sensation he felt in his stomach when the elevator descended rapidly. *I've seen too many movies where the elevator plummeted to the basement,* he told himself.

He felt the car slow its descent and his grip relaxed a bit. When it stopped, he gasped and realized he had been holding his breath all the way down. The doors opened and the two walked out into the plaza.

"I'll grab our table," Justus told Harrison and rushed ahead.

The Rice Bowl was not busy. Harrison was in and out in no time. He carried the tray with two teriyaki chicken and rice bowls and two large Cokes over to their table.

"One of these days you're going to have to pick up lunch," Harrison said and sat down.

"Sure, but that would mean you'd have to grab our table and then wait for me. I know how much you hate waiting," Justus said and ducked his head pretending to be submissive.

"So, what was all that about this morning?" Harrison asked while he took the plastic lid off his lunch bowl.

"What?" Justus asked, remembering the confrontation in the break room. *Surely Harrison couldn't have heard about that already.*

"In the conference room upstairs."

"Oh," Justus answered. "I recognized someone." He took a bite of chicken and rice.

"Who?"

"Andy."

Harrison looked confused. "There was no one named Andy in the meeting."

"The guy on the end of the table?"

"You mean Dominic Russell?"

It was Justus' turn to look confused. "Is that his name?"

"Yes, he's the son-in-law of Concannon's CEO."

"Oh my God," Justus gasped. "He told Scotty his name was Andy."

"You must be mistaken."

"No, I'm not. I never forget a face; especially when it belongs to someone who was mean and nasty to my friend. He bought Scotty a drink and then took him to his house in the West

Hills and dumped him there."

Harrison shook his head. "Well, he's married and has two daughters. He's not gay. So I doubt he's your man."

"I'm telling you it *is* him. He's hiding something," Justus said.

"Well, they're all coming back tomorrow to continue our meeting. I don't want you making a scene and embarrassing them and yourself."

"Why would I do that?"

Harrison gave Justus *the look.*

"Fine," Justus said and stuck a fork in another piece of chicken.

They ate in silence, but the running conversation in his head was so loud he was sure Harrison could hear it. The voices were asking unanswerable questions and it was beginning to cause him to lose his appetite. He took a drink from his Coke.

"Say, I invited Scotty to dinner tonight. I hope you don't mind," Justus spoke up.

"No problem." Harrison shrugged. "Doug is coming over, too."

"Oh?" Justus said, purposely sounding suspicious.

"Don't start," Harrison said.

Justus could see Harrison's face begin to turn red even though Harrison kept his head down. Justus smiled.

After work, Harrison and Justus picked up Scotty and then stopped off at the store before finally heading home. Douglas was waiting for them on the front porch when they drove into the driveway.

"Sorry to keep you waiting," Harrison apologized while he unlocked the front door.

"That's okay, I just got here myself."

Justus knew Douglas was lying purely to be gracious. He looked too comfortable sitting on the porch swing for *just arriving*.

While Harrison and Douglas busied themselves in the kitchen, Justus set the table.

"Here you go," Douglas said, walking into the dining room, "a Jack Daniel's on ice and a Coke." He held out the two glasses.

"Uh, do you mind if I have one of those?" Scotty said and nodded toward Justus who took the Jack Daniel's.

Douglas shot Justus a surprised and confused look. "Sure," he answered and took the Coke back into the kitchen. He quickly returned and handed Scotty his drink.

While they ate, Douglas recounted his day working in the West Hills. "I never realized how narrow some of those streets are," he commented. "We had a couple flaggers directing traffic but when the cars would pass by the truck, I could have sworn there was an inch of clearance between us, tops."

Harrison kept the topic going, "Anyone who lives there has to be crazy. The majority of those houses are built on stilts. With the amount of rain we get it's only a matter of time before they all start sliding down."

Justus looked at Scotty who appeared to be taking it well. He had thought talk about the West Hills would have made him more uncomfortable. However, seeing that it had not, Justus interjected.

"Scotty said that Andy lives there."

Scotty looked up with wide eyes.

"Andy?" Douglas asked.

Justus opened his mouth to answer but Scotty jumped in. "A guy who bought me a drink a few weeks ago. He took me to his house in the West Hills. Then he got all weird and upset because I wouldn't do him and threw me out of his house. Justus had to come pick me up."

"Only, his name isn't really Andy," Justus spoke up and looked at Harrison. "His real name is Dom—"

"Dominic Russell," Harrison said. "I don't think we should be talking about clients at dinner."

"He's not my client," Justus scoffed. "Besides, we're not talking about his business."

"Why would he say his name was Andy?" Scotty thought out loud.

"Maybe he was trying to keep his personal life separate from his regular life?" Douglas speculated. "Or he's still in the closet."

"Harry said he's married and has kids," Justus said and looked at Harrison who did not appear pleased with the direction of the conversation.

"Interesting," Douglas said and raised an eyebrow.

"Not really," Harrison said.

"Well, I don't care what his name is," Scotty spoke up. "I hope I never see him again. The man is a psychopath."

"Let's change the subject, shall we?" Harrison begged.

"Fine," Justus said. "Today in the break room I overheard some assholes talking about an article in the paper that said another man has gone missing."

"Really? Who?" Scotty looked across the table at Justus.

"Don't know. I didn't see the paper."

"Well, it's over there on the table by the front door," Harrison said.

Justus jumped up from the table and retrieved the paper. He unfolded it and opened it, scanning the articles.

"Here it is," he announced. "Friends report that Patrick Yarborough was last seen leaving CC's, a local country-western nightclub downtown which caters to the gay community, with an unidentified male. Witnesses could not give a definite description of the man and no one has heard from Yarborough since. Police have yet to comment, stating it is an ongoing investigation.

"Oh my god!" Justus gasped and lowered the paper.

"Wasn't that the guy you said saw who abducted that other guy?" Scotty asked.

"Yes," Justus answered. He dropped back into his seat at the end of the table. "Curtis said he didn't go out anymore."

"How odd," Harrison said.

"Was there anything more?" Scotty asked.

"That was all, only a small paragraph. Hardly worth anyone's time writing it." Justus took a gulp of his drink. "With the government finally acknowledging the rights of gays in this country, you'd think the police and media would follow suit. It's obvious they're still biased and homophobic."

"That's harsh," Douglas spoke up.

"But it's true," Justus said. "Those pompous assholes, excuse my language," he said, noticing Harrison's disapproving look, "were nothing less. It was infuriating. They compared us to Sodom and Gomorrah."

"Well, what can you or anyone do about it?" Harrison said sympathetically.

They finished their meal in near silence. Douglas attempted several times to start another conversation but each time it fell flat. Finally, he gave up.

When the clock in the corner of the dining room struck ten, Scotty stretched and yawned.

"I guess I should be going. I have to work in the morning," he said.

"We all do," Harrison agreed and swallowed the last of

his wine.

"I can take you home after I clear the table," Justus offered.

"Don't worry about that. Doug and I can take care of it. You two go ahead."

"Are you sure?" Justus asked Harrison and eyed the two of them.

"Yes," Harrison said. "And I know what you're thinking, so stop it."

"What?" Justus feigned innocence and laughed.

"Thank you for the wonderful dinner," Scotty said and stood up from the table.

"My pleasure," Harrison answered.

After grabbing their jackets from the coat tree in the foyer, Justus and Scotty headed for Justus' car parked against the curb in front of the house.

"So, are those two finally a couple?" Scotty asked.

"No. They're just old friends," Justus said. "But I still love teasing Harry. He gets so red when he's embarrassed."

They climbed into the car. Glancing over his shoulder, Justus pulled out into the street and headed toward downtown.

"I can't believe Andy would lie about his name," Scotty said out of the blue. "Don't you think it's odd?"

"Yeah," Justus agreed and wondered why Scotty was bringing him up again after barely saying anything earlier.

"I mean, because I told him I didn't want to have sex, he went nuts and threw me out in the street in the middle of the night. What sane person acts like that?"

"I don't know. I've never said no to anyone before," Justus responded and then his words sank in. "That sounded a little trashy didn't it?"

"Yeah, a bit," Scotty agreed. "You're such a little slut,"

he teased and they both laughed.

Justus pulled up to the curb outside Scotty's apartment building and parked. The vibration from the engine jiggled the steering wheel to let him know he was using up his fuel.

"Thanks again for dinner and the ride," Scotty said. He gave Justus a sideways hug and kiss on the cheek before sliding out of the car.

"No problem."

"Talk to you tomorrow." Scotty closed the passenger door behind him and waved while Justus put the car in gear and pulled away from the curb.

On the drive home Justus' past words echoed in his ears. It was true, he had never said no to any guy wanting sex. He used to be able to count on one hand the number of guys he had been with, but that was a long time ago. Sitting at a stop light on E Burnside, he began to list off the names of all of his hookups. *Marcus, Jack, Matthew, Luke, James, Jason, Steve, Brian, Brad or was it Brad then Brian*? "No, Byron. That was his name," he said out loud. The light turned green and he stepped on the accelerator while he continued to list names.

When he reached NE 14th Avenue he zigged left and then right onto Sandy Boulevard and headed northeast toward the Hollywood District. Somewhere in the change of direction he lost count and found he was counting the passing cars instead.

"Damn it!" he said and slapped the steering wheel. He slowed to a stop at another red light. "I guess Scotty's right, I am a slut." His shoulders slumped. He looked to the right through the windshield and noticed a man standing beneath a street light waiting for the bus. In the dim light, Justus' heart began to beat a little faster. The man looked rugged, like the Marlboro cowboy from the ads in his old Blue Boy magazines. He felt a stirring in his groin and wished the handsome man would look at him. "What are you doing?" he scolded himself. "Get a grip, Justus!" The light changed; he stepped on the gas pedal and left the Marlboro man behind.

Pulling up to the curb in front of the house, Justus turned off the engine and sat in his car. He looked at the old, two-story Portland Craftsman house and noticed Douglas' truck was now parked in the driveway beside Harrison's Honda CR-V. For a moment he wished he could be more like Harrison, having guy friends and not wanting to have sex with them.

"Where's the fun in that?" he said and shook the thought from his head.

He opened the door and stepped out into the chilly night air. The neighbor's dog began barking. He resisted the urge to yell at him to shut up and instead hurried into the house.

CHAPTER SIXTEEN

The morning commute into downtown Portland was quiet. Justus stared out the passenger side window while Harrison drove the two of them to work. He could not stop thinking about his conversation with Scotty the night before.

"Harry, do you think I'm a slut?" he asked.

Harrison let out an awkward chuckle and glanced at Justus. His smile faded instantly when their eyes met.

"Where'd that come from?" he asked. "Is that what's been bothering you since you came home last night?"

"Yes," Justus answered.

"What happened? Did Scotty and you have a fight?"

"No. I've been doing some thinking," Justus answered. "Last night in the car, Scotty brought up Andy. He's really bothered by the way Andy threw him out because he, Scotty, didn't want to rush into sex with him. He asked me what I thought."

"What did you tell him?"

"I told him I've never been in that situation before because I've never said no to a guy."

"I see."

"Does that make me a slut?"

"I honestly don't know, Justus. A bit promiscuous maybe, but I've honestly never thought of you with that term."

"Same thing," Justus said. "It's just a fancier word." He turned and looked out the window again.

"Hold it," Harrison said, glancing back and forth between the road ahead and Justus. "What's this really about?"

Justus looked at Harrison and tears filled his eyes. "I was thinking. I'm so not like you. I don't have any *real* guy friends, guys I haven't slept with."

"Yes, you do," Harrison said. "What about Dale, Marcus, and Jack?" He glanced at Justus and his expression drooped. "You didn't?"

Justus frowned and shrugged his shoulders a little.

"Well, I know you haven't slept with Scotty."

"True."

"So, there's one, and you haven't slept with me or Douglas. Don't say it!" Harrison warned playfully.

Justus lowered his head.

"So you have three male friends."

"If you say so."

"I do, Justus. Friends come and go—no pun intended, get your mind out of the gutter."

"I didn't say anything," Justus protested and tried not to grin.

"The point is, people will pass through your life constantly. Today you have Scotty and Dale in your circle of friends. One day you may add someone else to that circle or one of them will move away. Life is constantly changing. You don't still hang out with the same group you did in grade school, do you?"

"No, I guess not."

"What about high school?"

"No."

"See, your circle has already changed."

"But they didn't disappear or die," Justus said and felt his mood sink again.

"True. Justus, what's happening is a lot to deal with, but you're strong, energetic, fun to be around. All things that will draw others to you. You *will* survive. Isn't that one of those old songs from the '70s you listen to?"

Justus smiled. He loved that song. *Who says disco is dead?*

"Thanks, Harry," Justus said. He leaned over and planted a kiss on Harrison's cheek.

"Hey! Hey! Driving here," Harrison protested.

Justus smiled and settled back in his seat.

Minutes later, when Harrison pulled into his parking space on the third floor of the parking garage on SW Fourth Avenue between Oak Street and Pine, Justus reached into the back seat and grabbed his backpack. He reached for the door handle but Harrison grabbed his arm.

"I don't mean to bring up a sore subject but I'll be in a meeting this morning with the reps from Concannon Industries again. So you may see this Andy-Dominic guy around."

"Whatever." Justus shrugged. "Not my concern."

"Good," Harrison said and slapped Justus on the back.

Alone in his file room, Justus sat at his desk. He tried to concentrate on his proposal for a newer, simpler filing system but Harrison's reminder about his meeting and Andy kept crowding its way into his thoughts. He pushed away from the computer on his desk and rocked back in his chair.

It's just too quiet. Maybe if I listen to some music. . .

He reached over and pressed the play button on his CD player. The room instantly filled with the melodic, catchy lyrics and heavy, vibrating beat that brought up memories of happier times and lifted his spirits. He stood up and started dancing and gyrating while he went about refiling the loose folders.

"Sounds like a party in here," an unfamiliar male voice cut through the music.

Justus jumped and quickly turned down his player. He looked at the man in the doorway and went numb.

"What are you doing here?" he asked.

Andy smiled and walked into the room. He stopped when he reached the empty desk.

"I wanted to thank you for not making a scene up there yesterday," he said quietly.

"I thought I did," Justus answered in a curt tone. "So, what is your real name? I know it's not Andy like you told my friend."

"It's Dominic."

"Why did you lie?"

"It's complicated."

"Yeah, I bet."

"I know you don't owe me anything but would you do me the favor of having a drink with me after work tonight? I'd like to explain."

"Why?"

"I don't want to discuss it here. A drink would be more relaxing and I could talk more freely."

Justus' eyes narrowed while he looked at Andy, trying to figure out if this was another one of his lines. He wanted to say no, to tell him exactly what he thought of someone who cheats on his wife and how disgusting a person like that is but instead he heard his voice say, "Sure, I'm off at five."

"Okay, I'll wait out front," Andy said. He turned around and left.

Justus dropped down onto his chair and slammed a fist down on his desk. "Slut! Slut! Slut!" he said out loud.

"What's that all about?" Harrison asked from the doorway.

Justus jumped to his feet and took a step back, bumping into the file cabinets.

"Hey, it's only me," Harrison said and walked into the room. His dark-brown eyes looked concerned. "What's the matter?"

"Andy, I mean Dominic was just here."

"He was?" Harrison sounded surprised. He glanced over his shoulder and then back at Justus. "What did he want?"

"He wants me to go for a drink with him after work so he can *explain*," Justus answered.

Harrison looked a bit shocked and confused.

"I wanted to tell him, no but. . ."

"You told him you would," Harrison said and furrowed his brow. "You're not planning on fooling around with him, are you?"

"Oh, hell no!" Justus gasped and pretended to gag. "Rule Number Five, no sex with married dudes. Besides, he's not my type at all."

"So what will you do if he goes off on you like he did with Scotty?"

"I've got my cell phone. I can call a cab."

"Call me," Harrison said. "I'll come back downtown and pick you up. Where are you going for this drink?"

"He didn't say."

"I see. Well, let me know where and how it goes. Text me, call me, whatever."

"I will. Thanks, Harry."

"For what?"

"Everything." Justus smiled.

Harrison held out a handful of folders to Justus.

After Harrison left, Justus sat down at his desk and turned up his music. He glanced at the stack of mail in his in-basket and set it all in a pile in front of him. There were intercompany envelopes with file requests, junk mail from companies wanting to sell him new filing software and others offering sleek colored hanging files. . .

Justus stopped and held up a large envelope that was addressed to him and not the company like the other junk mail. He turned it over looking for a return address. There was none, only the embossed Hallmark stamped logo on the flap. He opened it and removed the card.

A cute bunny holding a large colored egg smiled at him on the front. Printed above its head was the corny line Hoppy Easter. Justus' heart beat faster as images of Dean's face flashed in his head. His hands began to shake. Although he did not really want to, he slowly opened the card; a loud pop caused him to jump while glitter and confetti bits showered him. "Mom!" he said as though she were standing in front of him. He read the message she wrote on the inside.

Gotcha!

> *I know I'm a little early but how else was I going to surprise you? This makes up for the Mother's Day card you sent me last year, the one that played that awful tune. It took forever for the battery to die.*

*Dad loves it here. He plays golf nearly
every day. I'm trying to keep busy but I miss
you and your sisters and I miss Oregon.
Write when you can.
Love, Mom.*

Justus stood the card up between his computer monitor and the framed photograph of his parents. He tried not to think about it too often, but he did miss his mother. She was more than just his mom, she was his best friend. He could talk to her about anything. Suddenly he had the urge to call her, to tell her about Marcus, to hear her say everything was going to be okay. He reached for his cell phone but stopped himself before dialing. The boss frowned on making personal phone calls on company time. He stuck his phone back into his shirt pocket. He would wait until he got home.

He sorted through the rest of the mundane junk mail and emptied most of it into the recycle box before he noticed the manila folder on the bottom. A feeling of sadness came over him. He opened the file and looked at Marcus' will. With a heavy sigh, he began to read it.

"Ready for lunch?" Harrison asked when he walked into the room.

Justus looked up from the last page of the will and nodded. "Sure."

When he stood up, glitter and confetti fell on the floor.

"What's all that?"

"My mom," Justus answered. "She sent me a booby-trapped Easter card."

Harrison started to laugh and shook his head. "You two crack me up. Let's go."

Minutes later, Justus and Harrison were seated at a table

in the Plaza with their steaming lunch bowls in front of them. Justus had managed to avoid picking up the tab again but Harrison did not complain.

"So, what had you so engrossed up there?" Harrison asked.

"I was reading Marcus' will."

"Oh," Harrison said and nodded to himself. "You okay?"

"Yeah, I think so." Though in reality, Justus felt as though he were slipping into a bad place inside. "I can't believe the luck some people have."

"What do you mean?"

"Marcus was twenty-five and he owned his own house outright. Where did he get all that money?"

"You're forgetting, Marcus lived paycheck to paycheck like everyone else."

"Yeah, but his paycheck was about double mine and he was a *computer geek*," Justus lamented. "I need a different job." He sighed and stabbed a strip of chicken with his fork.

"Well, if you're really unhappy with your job—"

"I didn't say that. I really like my job. It's not high stress and I'm not tied to a desk or a computer unless I want to be."

"There you go," Harrison interjected with a positive tone.

"But," Justus said, stopping him, "there are days when a little more cash would be nice. I mean, at this rate I don't think I'll ever own my own house or even a small condo like Scotty."

"If you had your own house, you'd have to move out," Harrison said.

"If I did, you and Doug could stop pretending and get married."

"Not happening," Harrison said and shook his head. "Neither of us is gay."

"In my world you are," Justus chuckled.

"Yeah, I know, in your world everyone is. But I've told you, again and again, Douglas has a lady friend."

"Whom I've never seen," Justus said.

"Well, she works nights and sleeps during the day."

"Works nights? Like a hooker?"

Harrison pursed his lips and gave Justus a disapproving look. "No, like a nurse."

"I hear some guys are into that sort of role playing."

"She's a real nurse. She works at Good Sam," Harrison answered, sounding a bit annoyed.

"Oh, my bad," Justus said and tried to hide his laughter. "So, what about you? I don't see you dating women—"

"I don't date men, either."

"So, what's that make you?" Justus continued to tease. "Oh, I know. I've got it, a monk!"

Another disapproving look.

"Come on," Justus whined. "That was funny."

"Not."

"Fine. I guess you're asexual, then."

"What?"

"Lacking sexual feelings and desires," Justus answered with a smile.

"Fine, if it will put an end to this conversation, I'm asexual."

"How positively dreadful and boring," Justus said and frowned sympathetically. "I feel so bad for you. You don't know what you're missing."

"I'm fine, Justus. Really, I'm not looking for a wife or anyone. I like my life. I'm happily single," Harrison said. He took a drink of his Coke.

"If you say so," Justus said and copied Harrison, sipping his Coke.

"I do. So let's drop it."

"Okay, we can talk about it later."

"No, we won't." Harrison said. "Now, let's get back upstairs before we're late."

Once they reached the twenty-eighth floor, Harrison returned to his office and Justus went back to his desk. He had rounds to make but he did not feel like it right then. Instead he pulled out his phone and called Scotty.

"Qwik Print. This is Eugene. How may—"

"Scotty, this is Justus."

"Hey there, what's up?"

"Not much," Justus answered and suddenly felt nervous. "Remember Andy?"

"Oh, crap, not him again. What?"

"He wants me to go have a drink with him after work. He wants to explain."

"Explain what?"

"Why he lied to you about his name. Why he treated you the way he did."

"Justus, I don't care what his reasons are. I don't want anything to do with him. He's such an ass."

"I know, but I sort of told him I would," Justus admitted.

"What? Are you freaking out of your mind? Why would you say yes? Oh, that's right. You never say no!"

"I wanted to."

"But you said yes."

"Yeah, I know. What do I do now?" Justus asked.

"Go for it," Scotty said in a tone that said more than the words.

"Are you mad?"

"No, Justus. I told you, I don't care."

"I'm not going to have sex with him. Only a drink and then I'm outta there."

"Like I said, I don't care."

"I know. I'm sorry," Justus said, sounding defeated.

"So, where are you going to meet?"

"I don't know. He's meeting me out front after work. I think we'll go to Stumptown."

"Well, let me know when you get home or if you're out late, you can crash at my place."

"I will," Justus answered. "Thanks, Scotty."

"Please, be careful. He's crazy."

"I will."

Scotty hung up before Justus could. Neither said goodbye.

Justus looked at his cart and then the clock on the wall. It was time to make his rounds.

CHAPTER SEVENTEEN

As the afternoon wore on, Justus felt more and more anxious about his impending drink with the man who called himself Andy. No matter how hard he tried, Justus was not able to stop time. He did not even have the man's number to call and back out of going.

"It's going to be okay," Harrison told him at three o'clock, again at four o'clock, and then again at four thirty. "You'll get your answers."

"But I don't care anymore. I should have said no. What was I thinking?"

"You were being a good friend, that's what," Harrison told him.

Justus paced the floor in his file room while the final seconds before quitting time ticked away. He wished he could be as sure of his intentions as Harrison seemed but he was not. Was he really about to break one of his own rules, he wondered.

"You ready to go?" Harrison asked, standing in the

doorway.

"No, but—" Justus sighed. His legs felt weak, like they did when the hygienist called his name at the dentist's office. He grabbed his jacket and slipped it on.

When they reached the first floor, Justus hesitated to leave the elevator.

"Come on," Harrison urged, holding the door open. "The alarm is going to buzz any—There. Happy? Come on!" The loud buzzing caught everyone in the lobby's attention. They stopped and looked to see what was happening which, judging by his red face, embarrassed Harrison.

Justus finally came out and Harrison released the doors. The buzzing stopped right when a security guard arrived.

"Everything okay?" the uniformed man asked.

"Yes," Harrison answered. He grabbed Justus' arm and pulled him toward the automatic revolving door. "It's going to be okay. Just have one drink with the man and then call me. I'll pick you up."

"Can I text you?"

"Sure, whatever you like. I'll keep my phone with me at all times."

Harrison practically shoved Justus into the revolving door before he followed. Both stepped out into the rain.

"Well, there he is," Harrison said and nodded at Andy standing near the corner of Sixth Avenue and Oak Street. "I'll see you later." He walked away leaving Justus alone.

Justus turned up his collar on his coat. *Of course, it has to rain.*

"Hi, you didn't tell anyone about us, did you?" Andy asked when Justus walked up to him.

"You mean, you, don't you," Justus corrected him.

"I suppose."

"Harrison already knows about you," Justus answered smugly. "After you dumped Scotty in the middle of nowhere that night, he stayed with me and Harrison."

"So, are you and Harrison a couple?"

"Why? What's it to you?"

"Nothing, just wondered," Andy said. He ducked his head against the rain. "Mind if we get out of this?" He held up his palm and caught a few drops in his hand.

"Sure, Stumptown is a few blocks up—"

"I thought we'd go someplace else," Andy said. "My car is right over there."

Justus hesitated. He remembered Scotty's warning. He knew Andy was crazy. He also remembered his rules about married men, *but there was something about him. . .* Justus looked at the cars parked along the curb while they headed up Oak Street and wondered which one belonged to the son-in-law of a CEO. Then he saw a sporty red Camaro and figured that had to be it. *Small man, flashy car.*

"Is that your car?" Justus asked and pointed at it.

"You like it?" Andy asked, sounding proud.

"Not particularly," Justus answered.

"Why not?"

Coffin cars. Get in an accident you might as well bury the car and its occupants. "They're too cramped and sit way too low compared with the other cars on the road," Justus said instead.

"Strike one against me," Andy said and opened the passenger door for Justus.

With a heavy sigh, Justus crawled in. The black leather bucket seat was uncomfortable. It poked him in the back and felt as though it could use some more padding on the seat cushion. He fastened his seat belt.

Andy had to wait for a couple cars to pass before he slipped down behind the wheel. He snapped his seat belt on and started the car up.

"I want you to know, I'm really a nice guy," he said while he pulled away from the curb and into traffic. "Your friend has issues, in case you didn't know."

Justus felt his jaw tighten. "If by issues you mean he didn't want to have sex with you—"

"Is that what he told you?" Andy asked and sounded shocked. "That's not what happened at all."

"Really, do enlighten me." The sarcasm dripped from Justus' every word.

"Your friend wanted me to take him to my place so we could be alone. I really didn't want to but he was persistent, so against my better judgement, I acquiesced."

Oh, using big words to impress me?

"Once we got in the car, your friend was all over me. I had to fight him off in order to drive."

This guy is so full of shit.

Justus looked out the window and realized they had passed over a highway. He looked around and tried to find a familiar landmark.

"Where are we going?" Justus interrupted another lie.

"I thought I would show you where I took your friend."

"Your house?"

"Yes. We can have a drink and talk in private there."

"What about your wife?"

Andy's head turned sharply and he looked at Justus in shock.

"Who told you I was married?" he snapped angrily.

"Watch out!" Justus ducked and yelled.

Andy turned and slammed on the brakes, narrowly missing rear-ending the car in front of them.

"Who told you I was married?" he demanded again.

Justus looked at him with an are-you-kidding-me sort of expression.

"Really? You're mad because I found out you're married?"

"Never mind," Andy said and gave a disgusted sigh. He stepped on the accelerator and they started moving again. "I'm not taking you to my actual residence. I'm taking you to my father's house. I inherited the place after he died. I haven't been able to bring myself to sell it, so I use it as a getaway from time to time."

"Does your wife know?"

"Never mind about her," he snapped again.

Ah-ha! Found your hot button.

Andy wound his way through the narrow streets of the West Hills as only someone who lived there could do. He followed Cardinell Drive to the place where Justus had picked up Scotty. Making a sharp left turn he started to climb up the hill along Rivington Drive. The road felt even narrower with parked cars lining the curb along the cliff side. Ivy-covered trees growing on the side of the road looked eerie in the dimming light of evening.

Justus put his head against the window and looked out, up the sloping hillside. High above them, he could see the houses perched on silts along the edge. Ahead, on the left, a house was built right at the edge of the road with only a narrow boardwalk that led to the front door. Andy swerved and missed the parked cars in the road.

"People have to be crazy to live here," Justus said.

"Crazy and rich," Andy bragged.

They passed three more houses on the left before Andy slowed.

"We're here," he announced proudly. He drove past the garage and turned off the road onto a parking pad that jutted out over the edge of the hill.

Justus gripped the door handle tighter when the headlights illuminated the drop-off at the end of the parking space. He looked up at the neighboring house set high above them. Lights illuminated the deck on the second floor and the underside of the house. Justus felt weak when he saw the two-story building appeared to have been built on poles that looked no bigger around than fence posts.

"Coming?" Andy asked and opened his door.

Justus glanced up at the deck of the neighbor's house and noticed someone watching them. He opened his door and stepped out, staying as close to the car as possible. He waved to the neighbor.

"Don't do that!" Andy snapped when he came around the back of the car. "Damn nosy neighbor. She moved in a month ago and I swear she has a telescope aimed at my house. Freaking bitch!" he yelled over his shoulder. "Mind your own business!" He took hold of Justus' arm and escorted him around the garage to the front door.

The front door was set behind what looked like prison bars.

"Security gate," Andy explained. "Had them installed after dad died. Didn't need squatters trashing the place. When I'm here, I usually leave them unlocked."

Justus wondered if that was another lie. Then he remembered that Scotty had been able to get out so he figured he was telling the truth.

Andy unlocked the front door and opened it.

Immediately Justus was struck by a peculiar odor.

"Oh," Andy said when he noticed Justus' expression. "My dad was into taxidermy. I hate that stuff and got rid of the worst of it. It stunk up the place so bad I think it penetrated the walls."

Justus did not say a word. He held his breath and stepped inside.

"Don't worry, you'll get used to it quickly," Andy assured him and closed the front door.

Standing in the doorway, Justus could see the living room, through the dining room and into the kitchen. The interior was decorated in a midcentury modern style that matched the outside but which Justus hated.

"My mother's idea," Andy explained while he hung his coat on the rack near the door. "She was into the modern, clean lines crap. Dad preferred rustic, cabin in the woods. I tend to lean his way but when mom died, dad didn't want to change a thing. Now, I'm stuck with it.

"So, pick your poison. I have a fully stocked bar." Andy clapped his hands and rubbed them together.

Justus choked and took in a deep breath that nearly gagged him. He pulled his jacket over his nose and mouth to serve as a filter. 'I'll have a Jack Daniel's on ice," he said.

"Coming right up. Make yourself comfortable. I'll be right back."

Justus watched him walk into the kitchen and open a cupboard. Andy turned his back toward the living room while he prepared their drinks. Justus slowly walked around the living room checking it out. Empty nails still stuck out of the walls. *Probably where Andy's father had hung his trophies.* There was a picture in a frame set on the mantle above a gas fireplace. Justus looked at the image of Andy posing with his wife and two daughters. *That takes nerve, keeping a picture of his wife and kids in plain sight. What a complete jerk!*

"Here you go," Andy said and handed Justus his drink before sitting down in the white leather chair across from the sofa. "Please, have a seat."

Justus sat down on the sofa. He took a sip of his drink and immediately noticed it did not taste right. The liquid burned its way down his throat. "What's this?"

"Sorry, I was out of Jack. It's an Irish whiskey. You like it?"

Justus held the glass up and looked at the liquid inside. It was clear like Jack Daniel's but had a paler hue to it. He took another sip.

"It's okay," he answered. "So, you were saying this is where you brought Ss–my friend?" Justus resumed their previous conversation, somewhat anxious to hear how his tall tale would end.

"Yes," Andy said and leaned forward, resting his forearms on his knees. Justus took another sip from his glass. "By the time we got here, your friend was a little more, shall we say, subdued. He wasn't all over me like he was when we left the bar."

"Uh-huh," Justus grunted and took another sip of his drink. "Do go on," he urged and tried not to sound taunting.

"Well," Andy stood up and walked over to the fireplace, "I fixed him a drink and then we sat on the sofa. I figured he was waiting for me to make a move. He was average looking and I figured why not throw him a mercy bone, if you know what I mean."

Justus felt his jaw tighten again and his anger start to rise.

"So, I leaned over and tried to kiss him, but he pulled away. He started screaming and yelling about how he doesn't fool around and that I was moving way too fast. I told him we didn't have to do anything we could simply sit here and cuddle a while. He demanded I take him back to the club. I told him I wasn't ready to leave yet but he was free to go. The next thing I knew that crazy bastard jumped up and stormed out of the house."

Justus tried to follow the story but something was wrong. He heard the words but they were not making sense anymore. He felt strange all over. Numb. He looked at Andy. *Why is he smiling at me? What's he saying? No! Don't touch me!*

CHAPTER EIGHTEEN

Justus opened his eyes. His head felt strange. He felt disoriented and slightly dizzy. He stared at the ceiling but was not sure what he was seeing. Slowly he rolled over onto his side. The plastic sheet beneath him crinkled. Justus looked at it and realized he was lying on a bed. The sensation of being cold swept over him, and his bare skin responded with goosebumps. He looked at himself and realized he was naked. Slowly he tried to sit up. A sharp pain in his anus sent a jolt though his body, causing him to lean to the side to take the pressure away. He put his hand down and ran it over the painful area. Raising his hand in front of his eyes, he strained to see it in the dim light. There was nothing. He was not bleeding.

Slowly he made his way to his feet, using the bed to support himself and keep from falling. His head began to throb and the feeling as if he were about to be sick bubbled up inside him. He looked for a wastebasket or bathroom, but quickly moving his head only added to his nausea. He sat still and took several deep breaths until the feeling passed.

Where am I?

He half sat, half leaned against the bed and looked around. There was a door on the wall directly in front of him. It was closed. Beneath the door Justus could see light. On the wall past the foot of the bed was a window with some sort of blind blocking out the sunlight. Still, a thread of light seeped around the edges. Behind him, on the opposite side of the bed, were another wall and window. Its shade was also pulled closed, but light seeped in through a zigzag lightning bolt that tore from the outer edge to the center, a telltale sign of a bad repair job. Nothing about the room looked familiar.

Why can't I remember? Where are my clothes?

Justus looked at the floor. There was something dark lying in a wad in the corner. Slowly he pushed off the bed and stood. His legs trembled and felt weak. He started to take a step but suddenly the floor rushed toward him.

When he opened his eyes again, his cheek was pressed against the cold tile floor. He turned his head and looked under the door into the next room but could not make out anything. He listened. Everything was quiet. He shivered.

Where are my clothes?

He started to push himself up onto his knees when he spotted something in the corner. He reached for it and grabbed the soft fabric. Pulling it toward him he sat down on the floor, bringing his legs around until he sat cross-legged. He held the fabric up and realized it was his jeans. He awkwardly shifted and twisted until he had them on. Warmth started to return to that part of his body.

While he sat on the floor, his jeans pulled up but not buttoned, the fog in his head began to lift. He remembered sitting on a sofa looking at Andy. His heart began to beat faster and his hands began to tremble. He tried to calm himself with deep breaths but only ended up panting. He began to feel dizzy.

What's happening?

He opened his eyes for the third time, but his memory of the first two times he had awakened was gone. He pushed himself up until he sat on the floor with his back against the bed and his feet stretched out in front of him. There was a ringing in his ears but otherwise the room was quiet. He remembered Andy looking at him and grinning. He had flashes of seeing his shirt torn from his body and of Andy pressing down on him.

I've got to get out of here.

Slowly Justus pulled himself to his feet. His legs felt a bit unsteady but they held him. He started for the nearest door, the one with the light slipping beneath it. He reached for the doorknob.

The sound of a bell ringing caused him to pull his hand away. It took him a couple more rings to realize it was not in his head. It was coming from behind the room's other door. Cautiously he inched his way toward it, steadying himself with a hand on the wall.

He opened the door to reveal a closet. It was empty except for a small wooden box on the shelf above the rod. The ringing sound was coming from inside. As his mind became clearer he felt his strength return. He grabbed the box. It felt heavier than he expected. He took it over to the bed and set it down. The ringing stopped.

Justus looked around. He needed more light. Walking over to the window with the torn shade, he pulled on it. The patch gave and the lightning bolt widened, letting light pour into the room. Quickly, Justus returned to the box and opened it.

Inside were several cell phones, wallets, a wrist watch, and a couple of men's rings: a wide gold band and what appeared to be a fraternity ring. Justus recognized one of the phones as his. He picked it up and tapped the screen. It illuminated but went black almost immediately. Two short beeps told him the battery was dead. He looked at the other phones. Their batteries were also dead. Dropping down on the bed and then adjusting himself to ease the discomfort in his anus, he picked up one of the wallets. He flipped it open and pulled out the driver's license. His heart skipped a beat when he saw the smiling image and read the name Jack O'Brien. He dropped the wallet and grabbed another. It belonged to Alexander. Another belonged to Patrick.

Police. I need to call the police.

Leaving the box with its souvenirs on the bed, Justus rushed out of the bedroom into a short hallway. For a moment he stood and looked around until he figured out which way to go. Once in the living room, he spotted an old olive-green phone on the kitchen counter. He grabbed the receiver, but when he picked it up it was dead.

The neighbor lady.

Justus ran across the living room toward the front door. His bare feet slapped the tiled floor. He turned the doorknob but the door was deadbolted. He turned the latch and threw the door open. The security fence was closed.

It's unlocked. The thought flashed in his mind. Was it a memory? Justus did not know but he rushed toward it.

A car screeched to a stop in the short driveway in front of the garage. The driver turned off the ignition and quickly jumped from behind the wheel. Justus' heart leapt and he fell back a couple steps.

Andy raced to the gate and used a key to unlock it.

"What are you doing out here?" he said through clenched teeth.

"I'm going home," Justus said with all the courage and power he could muster.

"I don't think so. I'm not through with you yet," Andy said.

Justus saw the small wooden club in Andy's raised hand but it was too late. He felt a sharp pain on the side of his head and then nothing.

The first thing that told Justus he was still alive was the excruciating pain that throbbed in his head. The pain was so intense it radiated down his neck into his shoulders and kept him from opening his eyes. The second thing was there was something hard in his mouth, stretching his jaws almost to the breaking point. He tried using his tongue to push it out, but it would not move.

Slowly he forced himself to open his eyes. It was dark again. The thick heavy scent of freshly turned dirt hung in the air and made it hard for him to breathe.

As he became more alert, he realized his hands were bound and hoisted over his head. His toes barely touched the ground beneath him. He twisted and pulled trying to kick his feet but a restraint wrapped around his ankles prevented him from moving.

Stay calm. Breathe slowly.

Following his own advice, Justus tried to take a deep breath but with his arms stretched above his head and the gag crammed in his mouth, it was hard for him to get air deep into his lungs. He started to panic.

Relax. It's going to be okay.

The pain in his head pulsated and caused him to close his eyes tight. When it eased a bit, he opened them again. He looked at his surroundings. There were thin slivers of light that formed partial rectangles along what he believed was a wall.

Boarded up windows.

He could not make out anything in the dark shadows around him. He choked and tasted copper.

"Good." Andy's voice came out of the darkness.

Justus twisted and tried to see from where.

"I was afraid our fun was over," he continued and stepped into view a few feet in front of Justus. He reached up and untied the gag, letting the black strap sag and the ball slip out of Justus' mouth.

Justus turned his head and spit.

Turning back to Andy's dark shape, he demanded, "Where am I?" His voice, however, sounded hoarse and weak.

"In my basement," Andy answered. "Well, it will be once I finish putting in the cement floor and sheetrock the walls."

"Help!" Justus shouted.

Suddenly the air rushed out of his lungs and a sharp pain burned his ribs. He gasped and struggled to get air.

"I wouldn't do that if I were you!" Andy growled inches from Justus' face. Justus could feel his hot breath against his cheek. "If you insist on being like the others, then we're not going to get to have any fun."

The memory of the box of cell phones, wallets, and trinkets flashed in Justus' mind.

It isn't Dean. It's Andy. He's the killer.

Justus turned his head away from the coffee-and-cigarette stench of Andy's breath. Andy's rough hand closed tightly around Justus' jaw and turned his face back.

"It's more fun when you're nice," he breathed.

Justus felt Andy's mouth cover his. Justus pursed his lips tight, resisting Andy's attempts to pry them open with his wet tongue.

Andy drew back. "Be nice," he snarled. He covered Justus' nose until he had to open his mouth to get a breath. At that moment Andy seized the opportunity and went in for the kiss. Justus brought his teeth down hard on Andy's lower lip and bit.

Andy shrieked and pulled away. "You bitch!"

Justus did not see it coming but felt the blow when his head was jerked to the side and his jaw cracked with pain.

"I have a mind to yank every one of those goddamned teeth out of your head. Where are my pliers?" Andy started looking around.

"No!" Justus shouted. "No, please. I'm sorry. I won't do it again."

Andy stopped and walked back over to him. "Promise?" he said but looked wary.

"I promise," Justus answered. He tasted blood in his mouth but was not sure if it was his or Andy's. He turned his head and spit it out.

Andy took hold of Justus by his jaw and turned his head until they looked each other in the eyes. "You really should be more cooperative. I don't like rushing," he said. Gently he ran his hand over Justus cheek and drew in for a kiss. Justus did not resist this time.

Out of breath, Andy pulled away and put his head on Justus' bare chest. "Wow," he said. "You're good. A lot better than that last one." He began kissing Justus' chest, moving down his belly.

Oh god no! Please don't let this happen.

Andy took hold of the front of Justus' jeans and undid the top button. A cell phone rang from somewhere above them. Andy stopped.

"Damn it!" he cursed and stood up. "I'll be right back.

Then we can finish." He turned away and disappeared into the shadows. Justus could hear the sound of Andy's shoes on wooden stairs. Moments later, a door opened and light from above illuminated Justus' surroundings. Andy had left the door open.

At last, Justus was able to see. The basement was not much of one. It was the underside of the house, with a rather shoddily framed wall enclosing the support poles. Sheets of plywood covered the outside of the framing, blocking out the light and the view of any nosy neighbors. There were places in the framing that Justus assumed were where windows would eventually go, but those too had been plywooded over. Still, there were enough cracks and spaces between the sheets that a little light seeped through. Even with what little knowledge he had of construction, the work did not strike Justus as being professionally done.

In front of him were piles of bagged concrete mix, a couple wheelbarrows turned on their sides, and a few five-gallon plastic buckets. Justus wiggled and squirmed, trying to twist around to see behind him but all he could manage to see was a mound of dirt to his right.

Upstairs he heard the muffled sound of Andy's voice.

"Can it wait? I'm sort of in the middle of something—Fine," he snapped. "I'll be right there."

Moments later Andy stomped down the wooden stairs, leaving the door above open. He walked over to Justus.

"Sorry, guy, this will have to wait; seems my *wife* can't handle her little bitch." He pulled the leather gag from his back pocket and stretched it out.

"No, please," Justus begged. "I won't yell. I'll be good."

Andy smiled and stopped. The leather strap was inches from Justus' mouth. He looked deep into Justus' eyes and lowered the gag. "You promise to be a good boy?"

"Oh yes," Justus answered feeling a glimmer of hope fill his chest.

"Are you sure I can trust you?"

"Yes. I promise."

Andy appeared to mull it over. The smile suddenly disappeared from his lips. "Why tempt you," he said and swiftly tied the gag in place once again. "I won't be long," he said while he headed back up the stairs.

Please don't close the door.

Andy must have been in a hurry. He batted at the door with the obvious intention of shutting it, but it only closed a few inches, leaving enough light that Justus could still see.

Once he heard the front door slam shut, Justus tried to free his mouth of the gag. Now that he had seen it, he tried wetting the leather strap by drooling on it to loosen it. His mouth started to feel dry. He pushed his head back between his arms, hoping to use them to work the gag free.

Once his arms were in front of him, he was able to look up and see that his wrists were cuffed. A thick chain was attached to one leather cuff and then looped around a heavy beam high above him before coming down to the other cuff. There was no way he could break it.

He tried for several minutes to free his mouth from the gag by working the leather strap down the side of his face but it was no use. Andy had secured it too well. He pushed his head back between his arms and looked down at his feet. Another set of leather cuffs were wrapped around his ankles. A rope, anchored on something behind him, kept them in place and prevented him from being able to turn around.

He thought about the ringing cell phone.

Please let it have been Harry.

Justus was unaware of how long Andy had been gone. At some point he had dosed off. When he woke, his arms and shoulders ached and his hands felt numb. He wiggled his fingers in an attempt to get his blood circulating, but he was not even sure they actually moved.

A sound of snapping twigs outside the makeshift wall caught his attention. There was a thud behind him. Justus pulled against his restraints and tried to turn toward the noise but failed. The most he could accomplish was to twist his torso slightly. A sharp pain in his ribs where Andy had hit him prevented him from trying again.

"Help!" he screamed, but only a muffled groan came from his gagged mouth. Still, he kept trying to call out as the sound of snapping twigs and knocking continued to advance along the wall, closer and closer.

Out of breath, Justus stopped screaming.

There was silence. Something outside moved in front of the sliver of light between the boards, blocking out the sun.

Oh my god, what if it's a bear? Justus' mind began spinning.

Whatever was outside moved but continued to block the light. Justus held his breath.

All at once it moved away and then there was a light knocking.

"Is anyone in there?" a woman's voice whispered loud enough for Justus to hear.

With renewed strength, Justus began to writhe and scream as loudly as he could. He pulled against the chains trying to make them jingle.

Something pushed against the weak spot in the wall where the light shone through. The boards bowed slightly and something that might have been the end of a crowbar pierced the gap, widening it. Justus looked up at the doorway above. No sign of Andy.

He looked back at his rescuer and pleaded with her to hurry but be quiet. However, the gag kept him from actually talking to her.

The boards creaked and groaned against the nails but finally began to loosen. A hand took hold of the edge of one piece of plywood and pulled, prying a section of it loose.

The sunlight that burst through the opening was blinding. Justus turned his head away and blinked, willing his eyes to adjust faster to the bright light.

He looked back at the opening and that was when he saw her. Like an angel surrounded in a halo of light, she leaned into the opening and looked inside.

"Oh my god," she gasped. "Hang on, son, I'll help you."

Justus felt his body relax. He watched while she tore another section of the plywood away.

"Almost there, honey," she continued to talk to him.

Her voice and her words betrayed her age. She had to be older than him. No girls his age ever called him son or honey. She must be old, Harrison's age at least, he thought. His eyes began to tear with relieved anticipation.

She tore the last piece of wood away and tossed it somewhere behind her. When the hole was big enough, she stepped through.

Once inside, with the light shining on her, Justus saw he was right. She was an older woman with amazing strength. Her white hair was cut short and permed. Her face bore the creases of time around her thin lips and dark eyes. Her mouth gaped when she looked around the unfinished basement.

"Oh my god," she said a little quieter than her previous

exclamation. "What on earth?" She walked past Justus, her eyes fixed on something behind him. He twisted and tried to see but pain and the chains prevented him from turning.

Justus grunted and shook his head in an attempt to get her attention.

"Oh, yes," she said and hurried back to him. She stepped in front of him and reached up to undo the gag. "Here you go."

There was a sickening thud, like the sound of a watermelon hitting the floor. The woman's smiling eyes changed to a blank stare. Justus looked down at the growing red spot in the center of her chest. She fell to the ground at his feet, revealing Andy holding a bloody pickax in his hands.

Justus' heart raced as fear gripped him.

"Now look what you made me do," Andy said in a tone that reminded Justus of his father's when he was disgusted. "You've been a naughty boy."

Justus shook his head and tried to explain but the gag prevented his words. Andy appeared to ignore him. He was too busy looking at the bloody pickax in his hands.

"Damn it!" he cursed. "Now I have to buy another one. I'll never be able get the blood off this." He looked at Justus and shook his head.

Andy tossed the pickax somewhere past Justus before he disappeared into the shadows under the house. There was the sound of metal hitting metal and then Andy emerged, dragging a large, old oil barrel with him. He stopped beside the fallen angel and took off the metal lid.

"This is your fault," he sneered at Justus. He bent down and picked up the body, dumping it headfirst into the barrel. He replaced the lid and pounded around the edges, sealing it shut. He wiped the sweat from his forehead and glared at Justus. Grabbing a shovel from the pile of concrete mix, he walked to the corner behind Justus.

Justus twisted and tried to turn to see what Andy was going to do but his restraints kept him facing away. He closed his eyes and bit down harder on the gag in his mouth. His teeth dug into the leather strap. He heard the sound of the shovel piercing the dirt. His body relaxed slightly. Andy was not going to strike him with it.

Andy seemed to dig for a long time. Justus could hear him becoming winded and panting behind him. When the digging stopped, Andy walked back into view. Dirt covered his clothing, and his face was streaked by sweat. He did not say a word or even look at his prisoner. Instead, he pulled the barrel onto its side and pushed it over to the hole. Justus heard the thud when it fell to the bottom. There was more digging, but this time Justus imagined dirt filling what he now knew was a grave.

The realization hit him instantly. Jack, Barry and the other guys from the clubs were dead. He pictured their lifeless bodies dumped into oil cans and buried like his angel. His legs became weak and fear tightened its grip on his chest with the understanding that he was next. He twisted and grunted. Tears filled his eyes and he began to cry.

Andy appeared in front of him. His expression was calm. His eyes seemed to express concern.

"There, there, now," he soothed and reached up to gently wipe the tears from Justus' cheeks. "It's okay. I took care of everything. No one needs to know." His tone was meant to allay Justus' fears, but it only frightened him more.

Andy reached behind Justus' head and took away the gag. Justus' gasps and sobs echoed around them.

"Shush, there, there now," Andy repeated while he stroked and caressed the sides of Justus' face.

"Please, don't kill me," Justus sobbed.

Andy froze, his hands still holding Justus' head. He looked angry. "Why would you say that?"

"You killed them, didn't you? Jack, Barry and the others."

"They didn't want to play nice," Andy hissed and glanced over Justus' shoulder and then back at Justus. "But you'll play nice, won't you?"

Justus nodded.

"That's a good boy." Andy gently slapped Justus' cheek. "I have one more thing to do. Then we can play some more."

Andy smiled. He turned away and righted one of the wheelbarrows. Grabbing a bag of cement mix, he dropped it in the wheelbarrow and tore it open. After emptying the contents, he turned to Justus. "I'll be right back. I need a little water." He grabbed a five-gallon bucket and headed up the stairs at a leisurely pace.

Justus heard whistling and the sound of running water. He looked around him and noticed the crowbar lying on the ground, barely inside the opening his angel had made in the wall. He wished he could get free. He would use that on Andy if he had to. Caught up in his plotting, he did not realize the water had stopped upstairs until he heard Andy's footsteps on the stairs.

"That didn't take long did it?" Andy said. He poured the water into the wheelbarrow and began mixing it with a garden rake. The sound of the rocks and sand scraping the sides of the wheelbarrow bothered Justus' ears and brought back memories of when his eighth-grade teacher, Miss Connors, would scrape her long fingernails against the chalkboard every time she used the eraser. It sent tiny bolts of electricity throughout his limbs.

Andy finished mixing the concrete and stepped between the handrails. He set the rake aside and picked up the wheelbarrow, wheeling it behind Justus to the grave. There was a swoosh sound as the concrete was emptied onto the ground followed by the sound of the rake smoothing it out. After three more bags of concrete, Andy finally stepped back in front of Justus. Sweat drenched his hair, face, and shirt. The stench made Justus want to gag.

"There, that should do it," Andy said. "You doing okay?" he asked.

Justus nodded and tried not to look disagreeable.

"Good boy. I need to clean up the wheelbarrow and then we can get back to business. All this heavy working has made me quite hot." He winked and pulled on a belt loop on Justus' jeans.

After retrieving another bucket of water from upstairs and cleaning the rake and wheelbarrow, the phone rang. Andy rushed up the stairs to answer it. Justus took a deep breath and let out a sigh of relief.

"Yes, I know what time it is." Andy's voice echoed down to the dungeon. "I know I promised to be home for dinner. Yes, I know how important this is for you. Fine, I'll take a quick shower—I told you I've been working on the basement in my dad's house—It was your choice to have this dinner party tonight."

Justus listened to Andy argue with someone that Justus guessed was his wife.

"I'll be home as soon as I can," Andy said and then was quiet. When he finally came back down the stairs he had a disappointed look in his eyes.

"I've got to go. You'll be okay here tonight. I'll be back first thing in the morning, I promise."

"I'm cold," Justus said, trying to sound passive.

Andy looked at him. "Oh, you poor little boy, let me see

what I can find." He rushed up the stairs. Justus could hear him in the room overhead. A few seconds later he returned with what looked like a blanket. "Here, this should work." He tossed one end of the blanket over Justus' head and moved it around until he found the hole in the center. "My dad bought this old poncho in Mexico on one of his trips," Andy explained.

The weight of the heavy wool poncho pulled on his shoulders and wrists making them burn with pain. Justus cringed while the wool scratched his bare chest and back. He was not sure which was worse, the cold or being itchy and not being able to do anything about it.

"Oh, I almost forgot," Andy said and turned back around. He clumsily refastened the gag and kissed Justus' cheek. "Be a good boy," he said and shut the door behind him as he left, throwing the basement into darkness.

Justus woke shivering. He had no idea how long he had been asleep or even how long after Andy had left before sleep had overtaken him. What he did know was that he was cold, itchy, and had to pee.

Oh God, not now.

He tried thinking about something else but since he was not able to see or hear anything, his mind kept returning to his pressing need. He bit down on the gag and tried humming the first song that popped into his head but immediately stopped.

It's Raining Men? Really?

He tried again but had similar luck with ABBA's *Waterloo.*

Damn it!

He decided to think of something else and stay away from music. The pressure on his bladder was becoming unbearable.

He thought about Scotty and Dale and wondered if they

even knew he was missing. When they had last discussed the person behind the missing men, they had decided the culprit was Dean.

How could I have been so wrong?

Tears filled his eyes. Maybe he had been wrong about Dean. Maybe he was not such a terrible man after all. A little lovestruck maybe, but not a lunatic like Andy.

Images of Harrison flashed in his mind. Justus had gotten a crush on him the first day they had met. Harrison looked so handsome in his business suit. With his dark hair touched with gray and his broad shoulders, he looked like a regular Clark Kent. Several times Justus had to stop himself from actually telling Harrison how he felt, that he was secretly in love with him—

But now he'll never know.

More tears. The outer corners of his eyes stung and burned. He wiped his face on his upstretched arms.

Douglas came to his mind. Tall, strong, handsome Douglas. Harrison insisted repeatedly that they were only friends and that was fine, but every time Justus wanted to spend some alone time with Harrison, Douglas showed up. Justus would never admit it out loud, but he was jealous.

Justus shivered when a gust of cold air blew through the opening in the wall, interrupting his thoughts. The pressure was beginning to overpower his ability to will it away. Before he knew what was happening or could stop it, warmth spread across his groin and ran down his leg. The liquid stung his ankles.

"No," he groaned and threw his head back. Even though he was alone, he felt embarrassed. This was not the way he wanted to be found.

When it stopped running, the warmth quickly faded,

leaving him cold and shivering. His wet jeans no longer shielded his legs from the night air. Standing on tiptoes in a puddle of mud, he tried moving to find a dry piece of ground but with each movement, his wrists burned and his shoulders ached. He realized he could no longer feel his fingers. He pushed his head back and looked up, but in the darkness, he could not see his hands.

Somewhere in the distance outside, a dog barked. Justus' head lunged forward. He looked toward the hole in the wall and held his breath. A twig snapped followed by something heavy hitting the ground on the other side of the flimsy wall. Justus' heart began to beat faster. He thought about the recent news stories of wolves and cougars being sighted around the West Hills. He wondered if they could smell his urine.

He heard another sound, another twig snap, and then a grunt. Whatever was out there was moving toward the hole. Justus bit down on the gag. A faint whimper escaped his throat.

Suddenly a light beam flashed through the hole in the wall. Justus' fears reached a new level. Tears burned his eyes and stung the corners. The memory of the white-haired woman standing in front of him, eyes frozen in a blind gaze, blood spreading out across her blouse, flashed through his mind.

"Over here!" a man's voice called out.

There were the sounds of twigs snapping and footsteps running toward the opening in the wall. A hand holding a flashlight reached through the wall. The beam moved erratically around the basement until it shone directly in Justus' face.

"Oh my god!" the man gasped.

Justus recognized the voice. It was Douglas.

"Justus?" Harrison was there.

The light bounced around and he heard the sounds of people climbing through the hole, scraping against the rough edges of the plywood.

"Justus!" Scotty's voice. Scotty was there too.

Someone was behind him, untying the gag. Justus gasped and closed his dry mouth, trying to build up saliva so he could speak.

Harrison stepped in front of him. The beam of his flashlight aimed up at the ceiling at Justus' restraints. He started to reach for them when they all heard a door shut above them and footsteps moving across the ceiling toward them.

"Stay quiet," Harrison said. He grabbed Scotty and pulled him over to the space beneath the wooden staircase where Douglas had ventured. They shut their flashlights off right as the door above them opened.

"I'm back," Andy said and started down the stairs with a flashlight in his hand. He shone the beam at Justus' face and stopped. "How did you—" He moved the beam around the room. "Who have you got down here, huh?" he asked. "You had better come out, I've got a gun and I'm not afraid to use it."

Justus looked at the darkness beneath the stairs and silently prayed for them to stay put and stay quiet.

"I'm not going to say it again," Andy said while he continued to move slowly down the stairs.

"There's no one here," Justus spoke in a voice he did not recognize as his own. His throat was still dry and the sound was raspy.

Andy pointed the beam directly at Justus' eyes. Justus turned his head.

"You wouldn't lie to me now would you boy? After all, we haven't had our fun yet."

"No. No, I'm not."

Andy moved closer and closer, still searching the shadows and dark corners of the room.

Justus watched as the flashlight's beam dropped to the ground at his feet.

"What?" Andy questioned and then looked up.

In the dim light Justus could see Andy's jaw tighten and his eyes blaze with anger. "Liar!" he shouted and struck Justus across the side of his head. Lightning flashed behind his eyelids and his head jerked right so hard he heard his neck crack.

Andy spun around the beam of his flashlight barely missing the three beneath the stairs. "Come out or I'll kill him right now!"

"No!" Scotty screamed, giving them away. He rushed at Andy but tripped over something on the ground. He fell and hit the dirt hard. Justus fought to keep from giving into his pain and passing out.

"What are you doing in my house?" Andy demanded.

"We've come for our friend," Harrison spoke up.

"Well, I'm not done with him yet," Andy growled.

"Yes, you are, Dominic," Harrison said.

Andy shook his head. There was a hint of recognition in his eyes. "How do you know my name?"

"I'm Harrison Andrews."

"Harrison—" Andy stopped.

"Put whatever is in your hand down," Harrison ordered while he moved closer and closer.

Andy's flashlight beam was aimed directly at Harrison. Justus could see what he was doing. Harrison was trying to cast as big of a shadow behind him as he could, hiding Douglas' movements from Andy.

"I don't think so," Andy replied in a defiant tone. He took a step away from Justus.

In the dim light, Justus saw the small metal pipe in Andy's hand.

"It's not a gun," Justus called out.

Andy turned sharply and swung the metal pipe he gripped in his hand, striking Justus in the ribs. Harrison lunged at Andy, grabbing him around the waist and tackling him to the ground. They landed behind Justus, out of his view. The flashlight slipped from Andy's hand and spun around on the ground, causing a strobing effect that reminded Justus of the lights at Stumptown.

Douglas rushed the pair and Justus listened to the sound of fists striking flesh and what sounded like large barrels banging into one another. There was the sound of something solid hitting the outer wall and then Andy's pained groan.

Harrison came into view, stumbling to the ground. He scrambled to his feet.

"Harry, no," he begged him to stop.

Harrison ignored him and disappeared behind him again.

Justus heard the crack of a piece of wood and a heavy thud.

"Harry?" he called and twisted trying to see behind him.

Andy rushed past Justus, heading for the stairs with Douglas running right on his heels. He grabbed Andy by his shirt and sent him crashing through the banister to the ground below. Somehow Andy managed to get back to his feet. He crouched down, fists raised ready to fight. Douglas did the same.

Justus watched, heart pounding wildly. Douglas threw a punch. Andy ducked out of the way just in time and countered with one of his own. It connected with Douglas' jaw but Douglas seemed unfazed. Douglas landed his next punch square in the center of Andy's face, sending his head rocking violently back. Andy recovered and the fight continued.

Justus glanced down at the ground where Scotty lay. He

was just starting to stir.

"Get up, Scotty," Justus urged while the fight drew nearer. "Get up!"

Scotty climbed to his knees, still looking a bit disoriented. He glanced over his shoulder at Douglas and Andy. That seemed to bring him to. He stumbled to his feet and backed away, giving Douglas as much room as he needed.

"Where's Harry?" Justus asked Scotty.

Scotty pulled out his flashlight and aimed the beam at Justus's face, blinding him.

"Behind me!" he shouted.

Scotty moved the beam and then rushed to behind Justus, out of his view.

Justus blinked several times trying to see around the dark dot in the center of his vision that had been left there by the bright beam of Scotty's flashlight.

Douglas threw two quick punches that hit Andy in the gut and then the chin. Andy stumbled backward, falling on the bags of concrete mix.

Justus saw the rake handle at the same time Andy did. Andy's hand closed around it and he brought the metal comb end up while he pushed off the bags.

Douglas backed away. He looked around him apparently searching for a weapon equal to the threatening tines of the rake.

"Not so brave now, are you, big boy," Andy taunted and moved closer.

Douglas' chest swelled and his fists clenched tighter. Without any warning he lunged at Andy like a football player going after the ball. His arms grabbed around Andy's waist leaving him no time or room to swing the rake. They crashed to the ground by the hole in the wall. Justus heard a gasp and watched Andy's eyes widen and his mouth drop open. A dark fluid spilled out over his chin.

"Doug!" Justus shouted.

Douglas slowly pushed himself up onto his knees. When he did, Justus could see the bloody, sharp end of the crowbar protruding from the left side of Andy's chest. Douglas stood up and turned to face Justus. Justus recognized the look in Douglas' eyes. He saw the growing redness spreading down Douglas' shirt.

"No!" Justus screamed.

"Doug!" Harrison shouted and rushed into view right when Douglas collapsed to his knees.

The sound of heavy footsteps overhead caused Justus to look up.

"Help!" Justus screamed.

"Down here! Call an ambulance!" Harrison shouted and cradled an unconscious Douglas in his arms.

Justus watched four men in police uniforms come running down the stairs. Then everything went dark.

CHAPTER NINTEEN

Justus did not know which he noticed first: the beeping sound or the bright light shining in his face. What he did know was he hurt all over but felt warm. He tried to move his arms, but they would not budge. The beeping sound grew more rapid. Justus twisted and turned while panic overtook him. He let out a scream like a wounded animal.

A figure moved across the room toward him.

Andy's face looked angry.

"No! No! Stay away from me!" Justus screamed but Andy moved closer. "Help! Help! Harrison! He's gonna kill me!"

"It's okay. It's okay," the woman repeated in a calm voice. She touched his arm.

Justus looked at her hand and then back at her eyes. Andy's face was gone, replaced by his sister's gentle features.

"Tina?" he said.

"Yes, I'm here," she answered with a nod.

Justus turned his head. Sunlight poured through a large window to his left, filling the room with light. He looked down at his feet and realized he was lying in a bed. He saw his arms, from his elbows to his wrists, wrapped in white gauze bandages.

"Where am I?" he asked.

"You're in the hospital," Tina said. She smiled at him, but Justus could see the tears in his sister's eyes while she stood beside the bed.

"Try to relax. Take deep breaths," a nurse on the other side of the bed instructed.

"Hospital?" Justus repeated. The word did not make sense to him. He tried to remember.

"Relax," Tina said.

Justus felt her touch his arm. He looked down. His arms were by his side. He tried to move them but could not. His heart began to race again.

"Please, Mr. Reynolds, you need to try to relax," the nurse said, sounding impatient. "Take a few slow, deep breaths for me."

Justus looked at her and although nothing was making sense, he did as he was told. The beeping sound slowed. He turned his head to see where it was coming from and saw a monitor on a pole near the head of the bed. He started to relax more.

"Harry?" he said to the nurse.

"He's here, waiting outside."

"I want him."

"In a moment. We need to make sure you are calm first."

"I *am* calm," Justus answered, but the beeping started to become faster again.

"Deep breaths," the nurse instructed.

Justus inhaled, slowly filling his lungs completely and

then letting it out.

"Okay, I'll send him in." The nurse nodded to the other people in the room. They all turned away and filed out of the room. The last one to leave was the nurse, who shut the door behind her.

A moment later the door opened and Harrison peeked inside. He grinned when he saw Justus.

"You're awake," he said and came in the rest of the way.

"Harry!" Justus choked and started to cry.

Harrison rushed over to the side of the bed. "It's okay."

Justus looked down and saw Harrison holding his hand but he could not feel anything. Tears slipped down the sides of his face. "Harry, where am I?"

"You're in the beautiful Kaiser Sunnyside Resort," Harrison answered in a playful tone. He smiled but Justus could see he was worried.

"Yeah," Scotty spoke up from Harrison's right.

"Scotty! You're here?" Justus gasped. He had not seen him come into the room.

"Yes, I'm here. We had to argue with the paramedics in order to get you here. They wanted to take you to Pill Hill, but you have Kaiser Insurance."

Scotty's words were confusing, and too much for him to think about right now. Justus felt the side of his head throb with sharp pain.

"Harry, I—I can't feel my hands," he whispered.

Harrison raised Justus' hand and gave it a little squeeze. Justus shook his head.

"It's okay," Harrison assured him. "You will soon enough. You need to rest. You've been through a lot."

Justus was confused. He looked at Scotty who stood staring at him with a strange, sad smile on his face. He turned back to Harrison who seemed preoccupied with something across the bed. Justus turned and saw his sister was still in the room. She wiped the tears from her eyes.

"What happened?" Justus asked.

"Don't you remember?" Harrison asked.

"Remember?" Justus answered while he tried to search his memory.

"It must be the meds," Scotty spoke up.

"Yes, you're on some pretty strong pain medication, Justus," Harrison agreed while still holding Justus' hand.

"Oh," Justus answered and nodded. He yawned.

"You need your sleep. We'll wait outside," Harrison said.

"No! Stay with me," Justus blurted.

Harrison looked at the other two and motioned with his head toward the door.

"I'll wait outside," Tina said and turned away.

Justus could see she was crying which only made him more confused. He watched her and Scotty leave the room. He yawned again and looked back at Harrison. "You're here," he said and closed his eyes.

"No!" Justus shouted and woke himself up. The room was dark. *I have to get out of here!* He tried to move but his arms wouldn't cooperate. *No!*

A movement to his left caused him to turn his head despite the pain that shot up from his shoulders, traveling through his neck and out of the top of his scalp. A dark shadow slowly rose and drew closer.

"No! Stay away from me!" he shouted. His heart thumped wildly. He fought the pain and wiggled himself away. He bumped into the bed rail and was confused. "No," he whimpered when he realized he was trapped. "Harry!" he shouted.

The dark figure moved toward him faster.

"No! Stay away from me!" Justus screamed again.

"Justus," the shadow called his name.

The room suddenly lit up, and a woman dressed in blue scrubs rushed up to the right side of the bed.

"It's okay," she said in a gentle voice. She put her hand on his shoulder. "It's okay."

"Harry?" Justus said when he looked at the person on his left.

The nurse moved away to check the monitor and tubes connected to Justus' chest and arm. Harrison stepped up to the side of the bed.

"I'm here," Harrison answered and took Justus' hand. "You're safe. You're in the hospital, remember?"

"Hospital," Justus repeated. He felt his fear drain away. He started to cry. His tears stung his eyes and ran back to his ears.

"It's okay, Justus, I'm here. I won't let anything happen to you."

"You promise?"

"Yes, I promise," Harrison assured him "Hey, you moved." He smiled and took Justus' raised hand.

Justus looked at his hand. It was still a bit swollen but it was looking more familiar. He then turned to watch his right arm while he lifted it off the bed.

"That's enough," the nurse said taking hold of his arm and putting it back down on the bed. "You need to be careful you don't pull out your IV."

He looked back at his left hand, at the gauze wrapped around his wrist. "What—"

"The cuffs rubbed your wrists and ankles raw," Harrison explained. "The doctor put ointment on them and wrapped them so you'd be more comfortable."

"My head hurts."

"I know. I'm sorry."

The nurse stepped back up to the side of the bed.

"Let's get you in a more comfortable position. Shall we?" she said while she put her hands under Justus' shoulders and nodded to Harrison who did the same. "On the count of three, one, two, three."

Justus felt his torso lift slightly and slide across the bed toward Harrison and then down again.

"There, is that better?" she asked while she adjusted his pillow.

"Yes," Justus answered. He realized the pain had lessened, too.

"Good. If you need anything, simply press this button."

Justus tried to look to where she was motioning but could not see what she was pointing at.

"We will," Harrison answered for him. "Thank you so much."

Justus watched the nurse leave and then turned his head and looked at the window seat. Even with the curtains closed and the light dim, he could see the cushioned seat was empty. He looked around the room.

"Scotty?" he said, wondering if he had dreamt it or if Scotty really had been here.

"He's with Douglas."

"Douglas—" A flash. A memory. Douglas lying on the ground not moving. Blood. Lots of blood. The monitor beside the bed began to beep faster.

"Hey, hey, it's okay," Harrison said while he patted Justus' shoulder lightly.

"Douglas. He was bleeding. Is he—"

"He's okay," Harrison said reassuringly.

"Okay," Justus repeated and closed his eyes while he exhaled slowly. He opened his eyes and looked around. Even though the light in the room had returned to a dim glow, he could see light around the edges of the curtains. Another flash of memory. The scent of turned dirt. An angel.

"What is it?" Harrison asked.

"I don't know," Justus answered. "I— What time is it?"

"It's two in the morning."

"How long have I been here?" Justus asked and felt himself slipping away. He yawned.

"Just a day," Harrison answered. "Hey, your mom and dad are on their way up. I called them yesterday afternoon and told them what happened. Your mom told me to tell you she loves you."

"I love you," Justus murmured and closed his eyes.

Justus felt as though he was weightless and starting to float. He looked down and could see his feet barely touching the ground. Then the ground spun and dropped away. A stabbing pain in his side caused him to open his eyes.

The room was filled with light. He looked at the wall at the foot of the bed. A whiteboard with different colored words scribbled on it hung beneath a schoolhouse-style clock. A door to the right was ajar and even though the light inside was off, he could see a toilet.

"Good morning, Sunshine," a nurse said. She stood beside the bed with what looked a TV remote in her hands. She smiled while she held a button down and then let go. The bed stopped moving, and she tucked the remote between the bed and the bedrail near his head.

Justus stared at the woman. She was not the same woman

he had seen during the night, *was she?* He watched her while she checked the tubes and wires. "Feel like getting cleaned up a bit today? I hear you're going to have some special visitors later."

Justus looked at her confused. The fog in his head was lifting at the same rate his pain was easing but he still felt lost.

"Where's Harrison?" he asked.

"I had your friend step out for a moment. We need to change your bedding and give you a sponge bath."

"We?" Justus repeated. A man dressed in baggy teal scrubs walked into the room. In his hands he carried a set of white sheets and a few towels. He smiled at Justus when their eyes met.

Not bad. Justus thought while he looked him over.

"Think you can make it to a chair?" the woman asked.

Justus looked at her.

"I don't know."

"Well, we'll help you," she said.

Justus began to feel anxious inside. He pulled away when she reached to help him. "I need to talk to Harry," he said, his tone demanding.

"You can. After we're through," the woman answered and tried to reach for him again.

"No, I need to talk to Harry, now! Please," Justus insisted, raising his voice.

The beeping on the heart monitor increased. The nurse looked at the orderly and nodded. Justus watched the young man leave the room and a moment later return with Harrison behind him.

"What is it?" Harrison asked standing beside the bed.

Justus looked at the female nurse and motioned for Harrison to lean closer. Harrison complied.

"I don't want her to give me a bath," Justus whispered.

"It's okay, she's a nurse."

"I don't care. I don't want a *woman* to. . ." He glanced down at his groin.

"Oh," Harrison said and raised his eyebrows. "Okay, I'll talk to her."

Justus watched while Harrison took the nurse out of the room. The door was open so he could see what was happening, but they kept their voices down. They stood facing each other. Harrison spoke first and then the nurse glanced back into the room. The look on her face was not happy. She said something to Harrison. Harrison responded. The nurse held up her hands as if to surrender and then stormed away. Harrison shrugged his shoulders and returned.

"What did she say?" Justus asked.

"She's going to see if she can find a male nurse."

"She's mad."

"She's not happy."

"Too bad," Justus said, sounding unsympathetic. He glanced at the male orderly standing beside the bed. He looked a bit uncomfortable but he nodded as though he understood.

"That's what I told her," Harrison said with a smile. "Oh, I almost forgot. Your parents arrived this morning. They're going to freshen up and then be over to see you."

"You'll be here?"

"Yes," Harrison said and gave Justus' hand a squeeze.

A big burly man dressed in loud, colorful scrubs walked into the room. "Someone need a sponge bath?" he said in a deep baritone voice.

Harrison looked at the male nurse and then back at Justus. He grinned and looked like he was about to laugh. "See you later."

Despite his size, the burly nurse was actually a gentle giant. He carefully pulled the blanket and sheet down. Justus saw his bare legs for the first time and gasped. They were red and his knees were bruised and puffy.

"Oh, don't worry about that," the giant said in a kind voice. "You'll be okay. We're going to remove the bandages around your ankles. I'll warn you, they're pretty raw looking."

Justus nodded. He watched while the big handed man gingerly removed the gauze. He tried not to be shocked but the sight of his beet red skin where the shackles had rubbed against him made him pull in his breath.

"There," the burly nurse said. "We'll leave the bandages off for a while. The air will do them good."

The other male nurse, the handsome one, set a large bowl of water on a raised bedside table. He handed Justus a towel.

"You can cover yourself with this," he instructed.

Justus clumsily took the towel. He tried to pull the front of the hospital gown up but his fingers would not cooperate and every time he moved them, bolts of pain shot up his arms to his shoulders. His arms dropped to his sides.

"That's okay," the young orderly said. "Is it okay. . .?"

Justus nodded. He watched the handsome man unfold the towel and slip it beneath the gown and over his privates. Once covered, the nurse helped him out of the gown. Four round stickers with what looked like a button with a small wire sticking out of it dotted his chest and sides. Justus gasped when he saw the large bruise on his side.

"We'll be careful," the young man assured him.

With both men working together, they gently wiped him down with warm damp washcloths. Justus lay back and closed his eyes. Even though it felt good, there was just enough pain to keep him from embarrassment.

"Here, I'll let you do the rest," the nurse said and handed him a freshly rinsed cloth. "Wipe off your personal area."

"I can't," Justus admitted when the washcloth slipped from his hand.

"If you don't mind, I can do it for you," the handsome orderly volunteered.

Justus nodded.

There was nothing sensual about the way the orderly handled his task. He seemed very focused and unfazed while he ran the damp cloth over Justus' manhood. In a few seconds he was finished. He put the cloth in a plastic bag with the towels. After emptying the water bowl in the bathroom sink he took the bag and left the room.

The burly nurse pulled a pair of pajamas out of a bag that was sitting in the chair by the door.

"Your friend brought these for you," he said and held up the shorts and shirt. "I'll help you put them on."

While Justus sat on the edge of the bed, the nurse carefully slipped Justus' feet through the leg holes and slid the shorts up to his knees. "It might be best if you stood up."

"I don't know if I can," Justus said.

"Lean on me," the giant said.

Leaning against the nurse for support, Justus slowly stood up. The nurse carefully but quickly slid the shorts up. Justus sat down on the edge of the bed while the nurse turned around and grabbed the shirt from the chair.

"This might hurt a bit," he warned. "You have some broken ribs." After threading the IV bag through the sleeve, he went ahead and buttoned the front of the shirt for Justus. "Think you can sit in a chair while I change your bedding?"

"Sure," Justus answered.

The nurse wheeled the chair over to the side of the bed

and gently lowered Justus into it. He then slid the chair back and went to work on the bed.

In no time he had the bed stripped and the fresh sheets spread out smooth and neatly tucked. He turned back to face Justus and looked worried. "Ready to climb back into bed?"

"I guess."

Carefully Justus returned to the bed with the help of his giant. With the top half of the bed raised, Justus was able to sit up. He watched the nurse gather his things.

"Can I get you anything?" he asked.

"No. Thank you," Justus said and managed a sincere smile.

"I'll see you later then," the nurse said, but it sounded more like a question.

"Sure," Justus said but the nurse was already gone.

Justus looked at his freshly bandaged wrists and his red and blotchy hands. He wondered if they would ever work again.

The door opened and a young woman in light blue scrubs and an apron walked in carrying a tray. She smiled at him.

"Ready for something to eat?" she asked and set the tray on the raised bedside table.

"I guess so," Justus answered. He looked at the glass of milk and the plate covered by a plastic lid. The woman removed the lid to reveal a plate of mashed potatoes, sliced turkey, peas and carrots all covered in gravy. Justus took a deep breath, savoring the aroma of hot turkey and gravy.

"Enjoy," she said and left the room before Justus had the chance to ask her for help.

Alone, he stared at the plate of food. He saw the plastic utensils still in their cellophane wrapper. He tried to pick it up but the pain that shot up his arms every time he moved his hands or bent his elbow was too much to bear. He dropped his arms to his sides.

When he was about to yell for help, Harrison opened the door and walked into the room.

"Ah," he said seeing Justus' untouched lunch. "Need a little help?"

Justus nodded. It was strange having someone feed him as though he were a baby. He would have been more upset had he not been so hungry. He ate every bit of his lunch and settled back against his pillows.

"Thank you," he said while Harrison straightened up the tray and replaced the lid over the empty plate. "Are they here yet?"

"No, you still have time," Harrison answered.

"Harry, I'm sorry."

"Sorry? About what?"

"I was so sure Dean was behind the missing men that I forgot all about Andy. We suspected him too, you know?"

"Yes. Scotty told me. In fact, when I didn't hear from you, I called him. He's the one who led us to the house. We made it just in time it seems."

"Yeah," Justus answered. The vision of his angel's face flashed in a memory. "He killed them all, didn't he?"

"Yes."

"I saw him kill a lady. She was trying to help me."

"I know. She was a policewoman. The police had been watching the house for several weeks. They were trying to build a case against Dominic but. . . well, that's all behind us."

"Behind us," Justus repeated. He closed his eyes and drifted off to sleep.

A light knock on the door brought Justus out of his dreamless nap. He looked at the door and saw a large bouquet of colorful spring flowers enter. Behind it he saw the smiling face of his mother and tears instantly clouded his eyes.

"Mama," he said and held out his arms, ignoring the pain.

Janet set the vase of flowers on the table and wrapped her arms around her son. Tears damped his cheeks while he held onto her. She cooed in his ear telling him everything was going to be okay. Finally, she pulled free of his arms and sat down the edge of his bed. She looked at him.

"My poor baby," she sighed and put her hand gently on the side of his face.

"Hey, Justus," his father said in a softer tone than Justus was used to hearing from him. "You're quite the hero, I hear."

"Hero?" Justus answered. He looked at his father, Nicholas.

"Yeah, you caught this serial killer. The papers are calling him the Stumptown Strangler," Nicholas explained. He held up the newspaper, showing Justus the headline.

"Nick!" Justus' mother snapped. "Put that awful thing away. He doesn't need to see that."

"Nonsense," his father said but lowered the paper anyway.

"Stumptown Strangler?" Justus repeated.

"Yes," Nicholas nodded. "He strangled his victims after molesting them."

Another flash of memory. The dark basement. The musty smell of dirt. The oil barrels. The pile of concrete mix.

"What is it, dear?" Justus heard his mother's voice. It sounded frightened. He looked at her.

"Ah, there's nothing wrong with the boy, " Nicholas said and gave Justus shoulder a slap which sent streaks of pain shooting though his body. He pulled away and looked at the man beside him. His breath caught. His heart beat faster. Justus tried to focus on his father's face, willing the image of Andy to disappear.

Nicholas stood beside the bed, the rail hitting him right above his waist. He was almost six feet tall and stocky. His hair was as dark as espresso and so were his eyes. He sported a heavy five-o'clock shadow no matter when or how often he shaved. That gene had skipped over Justus. He thought he saw a tear in his father's eyes, but knew if he mentioned it his father would claim it was pollen, dust, or some other lame excuse, never because he was worried or cared.

The door opened and everyone looked to see who was there.

Harrison walked in and stopped, obviously surprised to see the Reynolds' were already there.

"Oh, I must have missed you in the lobby," he said.

"Janet wanted to stop at the gift shop," Nicholas said and nodded toward the huge bouquet on the table. "How's your other friend doing?"

"He's doing better. The doctors were able to patch him up and he'll be released tomorrow," Harrison answered.

"Any word on when this one will be released?" Nicholas asked and slapped Justus' leg which made him jump and sent shooting pain throughout his body.

Justus let out a groan.

"Be careful," Janet reprimanded her husband.

"In a day or two," Harrison said and smiled at Justus.

"Good, then he will be coming home with us. We'll need to get your things packed first," Janet said and turned back to look at her son.

"No!" Justus protested.

"But, Justus, honey," Janet said. "You need someone to take care of you."

"I'm fine, mom. I'm twenty-two. I'm not a baby."

"No one said you were, dear. We could have lost you. You need to be closer so we can watch over you."

"No. I'm not going. Harry?" Justus looked at Harrison for help.

"Mr. and Mrs. Reynolds, I understand your concerns, but Justus—"

"I think we know what's best for our son," Nicholas interrupted.

"I'm sure you do, but if he doesn't want to go. . . He's an adult." Harrison did not back down for which Justus was grateful. "Besides, he has friends here who are looking out for him."

"And doing a fine job of it from the looks of things!" Nicholas snapped angrily. "He's coming home with us and that is the end of it."

"No, dad, I am not," Justus raised his voice. "If you came all the way up here just to drag me back with you, you wasted your time. I am not moving to Arizona. I have a job and a life here."

"But, honey," Janet spoke up. "We only want what's best for you."

"Then leave me alone," Justus answered. "You and dad made the choice to move away from here to pursue your new life without us kids. So let me live my life the way I want."

Janet glared at her husband. "I told you I didn't want to move."

"Now is not the time for that," Nicholas growled. "Justus—"

"I'm not going and there is nothing you can do about it."

"We will see about that," Nicholas said. "Come on, Janet."

"Think about it, will you?" Janet said hurriedly while she

jumped to her feet.

"Mom, I've made my decision. I'm staying and that's the end of it."

His mom's eyes teared up again and she bent down and kissed his cheek.

Justus sat looking at Harrison who stood at the foot of the bed. He saw the worry and concern in Harrison's eyes and felt his anger and fear drain away.

"I'm not leaving," he reassured Harrison.

Harrison nodded.

CHAPTER TWENTY

The warm summer sun felt good against Justus' face while he sat in his wheelchair. The bruises and cuts had healed without leaving any scars, for which he was grateful. However, he still had shooting pain whenever he moved his hands and was doing physical therapy to help him with walking again. If only the nightmares would stop and he could get a full night's rest, maybe then he would start to feel normal again.

He looked up at Harrison and Douglas standing by his side. In his lap he held the small wooden box that contained the ashes of his friend Marcus. He looked across the small grave at Dale and Scotty. Scotty's eyes were red and wet with tears.

A woman in a lightweight, spring dress stepped forward. She held out her hands toward the box. Justus moved his cupped hands away, letting her take it. He watched her place it into the small white coffin-shaped container and seal it shut. She stepped away, leaving the coffin sitting on the larger box covered in fake green grass over the grave.

Justus felt Harrison's hand touch his shoulder. He looked

up at him. Harrison smiled and then looked at the gathering.

"Thank you all for coming," Harrison said in a loud voice that carried up the hillside of Skyline Memorial Gardens. "We are here to pay our respects to our beloved friend, Marcus Philip Morelli."

While Harrison continued his eulogy, Justus looked up the hillside at the flowers that covered a fresh grave. The mourners from that funeral were already heading toward the parking lot at the top of the hill. He looked back at the gathering.

"He was a bright flame that burned out way too soon. We will miss him forever," Harrison concluded.

One by one, friends stepped forward and placed a red rose on the ground in front of the green box. Justus watched Miss Scarlett and Cherry Royale step forward with their roses. Miss Scarlett looked every bit the southern belle: large brimmed hat with a bit of tulle draped over the edge, a formal full-length dress minus the hoop-skirt, and white gloves that went up to her elbows. On the other hand, Cherry Royale was shrouded in a long black veil, a black gown, and black gloves. It made Justus think she looked like a bride of Dracula. He looked away.

The crowd slowly dispersed, leaving Justus and his close friends alone. He spotted the gravediggers lurking under a tree in the distance.

"I think they want us to leave," he said and nodded in their direction.

Scotty stepped forward and placed his rose on top of the white coffin. He kissed his fingertips and pressed them to the top.

"I love you," he said quietly, but Justus still heard him.

Once Scotty regained his composure, the group moved up the hill toward the parking lot. Justus motioned at Harrison's arm as they neared the flower laden grave.

"I want to stop by Jack's grave and leave this rose."

"Of course," Harrison told him. He pushed the wheelchair over to the spot. Douglas, Scotty, and Dale waited a few yards back.

Justus drew a deep, quivering breath. He looked at the spray of red roses and white carnations that lay across the cut sod. A red ribbon was pinned across the arrangement, with Beloved Son written in golden letters down its center.

"I can't believe there were so many," Justus said. "How could someone kill so many people, bury them right under his own house, and it take months to find him?"

"He was a monster, for sure," Harrison said. "There's no other explanation."

"Did I tell you I spoke with Barry's mother?"

"No. When?"

"I called her a couple days ago," Justus answered in a disgusted tone. "I wanted to tell her how sorry I was about her son. You know what she said? She said she lost her son a long time ago when he decided to pursue a homosexual lifestyle. Can you believe it?"

Harrison shook his head.

"She said, 'At least he didn't die from AIDS and cause the family more embarrassment.' I wanted to reach through the phone and choke her. How could a mother say such a horrible thing about her own son?"

"I don't know."

"When I asked when his funeral would be, she told me they weren't having one and not to send flowers. She wouldn't even tell me where they had him buried."

"I'm sorry," Harrison sympathized. "Are you ready to go home?"

"Yes."

It took thirty-five minutes with traffic and stop lights for Harrison to drive from NW Skyline Blvd at the end W Burnside to downtown Portland. Justus sat quietly in the passenger seat and stared out the window while they crossed the Burnside Bridge.

"When should I tell Scotty about Marcus' will?" he asked Harrison. Justus glimpsed a handsome man in shorts standing at a bus stop, but he did not do a double take like he would have just a few weeks ago.

"It's really up to you, whenever you're ready."

"How do you think Scott's going to react?"

"Judging from what I saw today, you should expect more tears," Harrison answered.

"I don't want to upset him any more than he already is."

"Well, I think it will upset him no matter when you tell him. So, think about it."

"Should I say anything to Dale?"

"He's going to find out anyway."

"Yeah but he's going to be hurt. He's known Marcus for as long as Scotty has. I feel so bad for him that he wasn't named in the will."

"Hey, it was Marcus' decision, not yours. Dale can't be upset with you. . . well, he can but that's beside the point. The point is, if Dale decides to be mad at you, then that's his problem. Not yours."

"Still, he's my friend and I don't want to lose him. I don't have many left."

"I know. We'll get through this like we have the rest of it, one day at a time. Okay?" Harrison glanced at Justus.

"Yeah," Justus agreed.

"It's Friday, are you guys going to the club tonight?" Harrison changed the subject.

"I don't know. . ."

"Come on, you haven't been out in weeks. Why not go and have a drink in memory of Marcus?"

"I just don't feel like it. After everything that's happened, I just don't know."

"It's okay to be a little afraid because of Dean—"

"It's not that. Besides, he sent a really nice card when he found out about what happened to me and all. He told me he was being transferred to another job in Seattle."

"Maybe it's for the best."

"Maybe," Justus agreed.

"So, what is it? Why don't you want to get back out there?" Harrison asked and turned off Sandy Blvd onto Broadway.

Justus did not answer. He did not know how to express that he had become afraid of men, strangers especially. That every time he looked at them, he could not help but see Andy and remember what he did. Hearing about losing the Concannon account at work was actually a relief. At least when he finally was able to go back, he would not have to ever pull that file again.

Harrison slowed and turned into the driveway. Justus noticed Douglas' truck. Douglas had made a quick recovery from his serious surgery that had been needed after being gored by the same tire iron that stopped Andy. Scotty had been such a help to him, which had left Harrison free to dote on Justus.

Harrison parked the CR-V and quickly jumped out. He raised the back hatch and took out Justus' wheelchair. Justus opened his door and readied himself to be lowered into the chair. It had become less awkward the more he had done it. Harrison closed the car door and used his key fob to lock it.

Justus sat back while Harrison wheeled him around to the

front of the house. Harrison had a temporary ramp built so he could roll the wheelchair up to the front door. Once through the front door, Col. Mustard came running. He jumped onto Justus' lap and nuzzled his chin. He mewed a couple times before turning around and settling down.

"Crazy cat," Harrison laughed. "Let me know if you want him down.

"He's fine for now," Justus said and gave Col. Mustard an awkward pat on the head with his semi-closed fist. "Have you guys been waiting long?"

"Not too long," Scotty said and stood up from where he had been sitting on the couch next to Douglas. "Want a drink or something to eat? I can't believe how nice people have been. When we got back here, there was a couple just leaving the front porch. They said they were neighbors and wanted to help out. They handed me a pan of homemade lasagna. I put it in the kitchen with the rest of the food."

"Thanks," Harrison acknowledged.

"I'll have a Coke," Justus said. "Still taking meds. Can't have any alcohol."

"I think one drink wouldn't hurt," Harrison spoke up.

"Okay, put a little Captain Morgan's in it."

"Coming right up," Scotty said, sounding more like his old self. "How about you, Harry?"

"I was hoping I could coax Douglas into making one of his coffee nudge drinks," Harrison answered.

"Sure thing," Douglas said. He jumped up and headed for the kitchen.

Col. Mustard began to squirm. Harrison picked him up and put him on the floor. He quickly trotted off to somewhere in the back of the house.

"So, what have you two been doing?" Justus asked and

wheeled himself up to the dining room table.

Douglas shrugged his shoulders. "Nothing. Just waiting for you two."

Justus eyed him suspiciously.

"Don't start," Harrison warned and sat down in his usual place at the table.

"I wasn't going to say anything." Justus feigned innocence and laughed.

Just then Dale walked into the room from the hall. He was still wiping his hands on his slacks. "I thought I heard you guys," he said.

"You do know there's a towel hanging on the hook beside the sink," Harrison said to him.

"Oh yeah, I saw but it's a habit."

"Here you go," Scotty said when he returned. He handed Justus a glass.

"Thanks." He took a sip. The spiced rum blended with the cola and tasted good.

"So, what is the plan for the evening?" Douglas asked when he walked back into the room. He set a mug in front of Harrison before retrieving his and Scotty's drinks from the living room.

"I guess we could order pizza and watch a movie," Harrison suggested.

"Isn't it your club night," Douglas said, prodding the three and dropping a hint.

"I don't think I can—"

"Nonsense," Douglas said. "Just because you're in that chair doesn't mean you can't have fun."

Justus looked at Dale and then Scotty.

"What can it hurt?" Scotty said and gave a purposeful nod.

"Jack and Marcus would have wanted us to," Dale agreed.

"Then it's settled," Harrison interjected.

"Does that mean you both are coming too?" Justus asked and looked at Harrison and then at Douglas.

Douglas turned to Harrison. "Sure, why not?" Douglas answered.

"Harry?" Justus asked.

"If it means that much to you, fine," Harrison answered. "But just this once and I don't want to hear about it again."

"I promise," Justus said and grinned.

ABOUT THE AUTHOR

Author A. M. Huff was born and raised in the Pacific Northwest. At an early age he aspired to be a writer and over the next thirty years, he continued to write with the encouragement of friends and relatives.

After retiring early from his day job, he joined a writers' group and began down the path to publication. *Ellensburg* is the first of a series of suspense/thriller novels.

For more about A. M. Huff visit his website: amhuff.com

If you've enjoyed this story, please leave a review on Amazon.com or Goodreads.com.